"I Heard In Town You Need A Foreman."

Startled, Rose looked up into Sullivan's eyes.

He saw the denial before she even opened her mouth. He had expected no less.

Rose knew if she had any sense, she would ignore him, tell him no. But she was seven-and-a-half-months pregnant. There was no avoiding the fact that soon she wouldn't be able to run the ranch at all. Like it or not, she had to find a foreman. Soon.

Which brought her back to Sullivan.

"I suppose you heard why I fired the last foreman?"

Sullivan shrugged carelessly. "He made a pass. You objected. What has that got to do with me? All I want is a job." *For now.* "Do I have it or not?"

Dragging in a bracing breath, Rose prayed she was doing the right thing. "You have it. You can start immediately."

Dear Reader:

Happy summertime reading from everyone here! July is an extra-special month, because Nora Roberts—at long last—has written a much-anticipated Silhouette Desire. It's called *A Man for Amanda* and it's part of her terrific series, THE CALHOUN WOMEN. Look for the distinctive portrait of Amanda Calhoun on the cover.

And also look for the portrait of July's *Man of the Month,* Niall Rankin, on the cover of Kathleen Creighton's *In From the Cold.* Ms. Creighton has written a number of books for Silhouette Intimate Moments. Please *don't* miss this story; I know you'll love it!

There is something for everyone this month— sensuous, emotional romances written just for *you!* July is completed with other must-reads from the talented pens of your *very* favorites: Helen R. Myers, Barbara Boswell, Joan Johnston and Linda Turner. So enjoy, enjoy....

All the best,

Lucia Macro
Senior Editor

LINDA TURNER

WILD TEXAS ROSE

SILHOUETTE *Desire*®

Published by Silhouette Books New York

America's Publisher of Contemporary Romance

SILHOUETTE BOOKS
300 East 42nd St., New York, N.Y. 10017

WILD TEXAS ROSE

ISBN: 0-373-05653-2

First Silhouette Books printing July 1991

LINDA TURNER

began reading romances in high school and began writing them one night when she had nothing else to read. She's been writing ever since. Single and living in Texas, she travels every chance she gets, scouting locales for her books.

Special thanks to Billy and Judy Wallace
and John Jones from Kerrville.
And to my agent, Lettie Lee,
for always being in my corner.

Prologue

The wind swirled through the granite tombstones of the old cemetery, scattering dead leaves among the graves. His shoulders hunched under his worn blue jean jacket, Sullivan Jones stared blindly down at the simple tin marker that indicated his father's grave. Bitter memories slashed at him, carving hard lines in his already chiseled face and pulling him back five years to the last time he'd seen his father alive.

As usual, they'd been arguing over the way the old man's drinking was driving the ranch right into the ground. They'd had the same argument countless times before, and it had always consisted of nothing more than hot words and curses. That particular day, however, Travis Jones had been mean drunk and spoiling for a fight. The only weak link in a long line of strong men, something had just seemed to snap.

When Sullivan had unwisely told him that his grandfather would turn over in his grave if he could see what he was doing to the ranch, he'd snarled, "To hell with you and your grandpa! For as long as I can remember, I've had to listen to one or the other of you tell me every damn little thing I do wrong. I'm tired of it, you hear? Get out!" Marching over to the front door, he'd thrown it open and ordered Sullivan off the premises as if he was a bill collector instead of his only son. "You get out of here and don't come back till I'm dead. Then you can run things any damn way you want."

His hands balling into fists in the pockets of his jacket, Sullivan's mouth set in a flat line as he remembered the way he'd stormed out. Twenty-six and hot-headed, his pride demanding that he take his father at his word, his one thought had been to get away. Before the day had ended, he'd left Kerrville without a backward glance and gone to San Antonio to join the marines.

It was a stupid thing to do in the heat of anger, but he'd signed on the dotted line and there was no backing out. Eating crow, he'd called his father to tell him where he was and make peace. But his father hadn't been interested in healing the breach then, or two years later, when Sullivan got out of the service.

You aren't welcome at the Lazy J.

Even now, Sullivan could hear the cold, bitter words whispering in the wind. Even now, he could feel the hurt and anger that had driven him out west, where he had moved from one ranch to another, working as a hired hand, all the while longing for Texas and home.

After three years he'd had enough of working other people's cattle, enough of long, brutal winters and short summers that were never as hot as he wanted them to be. He was through with the emptiness, the loneliness he could never seem to shake. His father could raise bloody hell for all he cared, but nothing was stopping him from going home.

But he'd waited too long. He had arrived in town just this afternoon only to discover that Travis Jones had been dead for over a year and the ranch was gone.

Pain burned like a branding iron in Sullivan's chest, each breath searing him. His stinging eyes as dry as an empty water hole, he lifted his gaze to the horizon and saw everything he had lost. His father, the chance to make amends, the land that five generations of Joneses had worked and sweated and died over. All gone.

He should have been here! he wanted to cry. He could have found a way to stop the old man's mismanagement of the ranch. And he damn well could have stopped him from going to Frank MacDonald for a loan when things got so bad even the bank wouldn't loan him money.

Dammit, how could he have gone to Frank for anything? he wondered furiously. The Joneses and MacDonalds had ranched side by side for decades, sharing a common boundary line, but they'd never been friends, never even been neighborly. Everyone in Kerr County knew the MacDonalds had always resented the fact that it was they who had the much smaller spread and seemed to stand in the shadow of the Lazy J. And Frank was the worst of the lot.

For as long as Sullivan could remember, Frank had coveted everything Sullivan had—toys when they were younger, then horses, cars, women. And always the ranch. How he must have laughed with glee when Travis Jones showed up on his doorstep with his hand out. He'd only had to wait for the first missed loan payment to snatch the ranch right out from under his nose.

A month later his father died a lonely, broken man, his old drinking buddies the only people at his funeral because no one had had any idea where his only son was. For no other reason than that, he would have given anything to have five minutes alone with Frank MacDonald.

But that, too, was to be denied him. Frank was dead, killed six months ago by a fall from his horse. There was no one left to get revenge from. No one except Rose, Frank's widow. The girl Sullivan had left behind when he'd joined the marines. The girl who'd married his worst enemy before he had even finished boot camp. The woman who now, at the tender age of twenty-three, had inherited not only Frank's ranch, but his, as well.

Somehow he was going to make her pay.

One

Rose MacDonald cast a quick, anxious look over her shoulder at the dark, bruised clouds hovering on the horizon, silently gathering strength. By nightfall the full force of the late winter cold front was expected to sweep unrestricted across the Texas Hill Country, bringing freezing rain and sleet with it. The temperature, already in the mid-thirties, would drop to near zero.

Hurry. Urgency tingled on the cold wind that whipped around her, threatening to tear her blue knit cap from her head. Tugging it back in place over her dark curls, she knew she was running out of time. She had food and supplies to get in town, extra feed to pull out for the cattle, supper to cook. The only three ranch hands she had were scattered over her vast spread, battening down the hatches for the icy weather, and somewhere in the east pasture a fence was down. Sometime between now and darkness she'd have to find time to fix it herself.

She groaned at the thought. The weight of the responsibility on her shoulders seemed to grow heavier with each passing day. Ever since she'd been forced to fire Buck Hastings, her foreman, she'd known she couldn't handle the ranch alone. She should have hired someone to replace him immediately, but too many of the cowboys who had approached her about the job had looked her over as if they were more interested in taking her over rather than her ranch if she made the mistake of trusting them.

But trust didn't come easy to her. Not now. Not after years of being manipulated by the men in her life without her even realizing it. Wincing at the memories that slapped her in the face, she wondered how she could have been so blind, so naive. Her mother died when she was seven, and she was so terrified of being alone that she childishly thought the safety and security of her world depended solely on her ability to please her father. It never entered her head that he might use her fears and her need to please to control her. For years he subtly influenced what she thought, how she dressed, who she made friends with. He even went so far as to pick out a rich husband for her—Frank MacDonald—and she never thought to buck him. Then she met Sullivan Jones.

And fell in love.

Lawrence Kelly detested him on sight. He wanted her to marry money, and although the Jones name was synonymous with ranching in Texas, the family fortunes were on the decline. To add insult to injury, Sullivan was a man her father knew he would never be able to control. By nothing more than his silence, he made his disapproval clear.

But for Sullivan she would have been willing to defy the world and her father. She never got the chance. He took her from innocence to passion, then left town without a word of explanation or goodbye.

After that, nothing seemed to matter. Her father stepped up his efforts to push her into Frank's arms, and she couldn't find the energy to fight him. A month after Sullivan disappeared from her life forever, her father had a heart attack and died hours later. On his deathbed he pleaded with her to accept Frank's proposal, claiming he could die happy knowing she wasn't alone. Her world caving in on her, she buckled under the weight of the guilt trip and gave in.

Young and trusting and sick at heart, she never thought to question Frank's reasons for wanting to marry her. Although he had never said the words, she'd assumed he loved her. It wasn't until five years later and a week after Frank's funeral, on the day she fired Buck Hastings, that she learned the truth. Just before he walked out with most of her ranch hands, Buck viciously told her that she'd never been anything but a means to an end for Frank, the weapon he was going to use against the only man in the world he hated...Sullivan Jones. For years he'd dreamed of building a dynasty that would one day equal, then surpass that of the Joneses. What better way to do it than with Sullivan's woman and his ranch?

She winced, trying once again to convince herself that Buck was lying. But his words had carried a ring of truth to them and the bitter sting of betrayal. All lies, she thought numbly. She'd been taken in by lies, used by opportunists, her self-worth stomped on until it was in shambles. But that was all in the past. At the moment there was only one male in her life she cared about.

Shivering, her cheeks already chapped, she buried her gloved hands deep in the pockets of Frank's old plaid coat and struggled to find her patience as she surveyed Bubba, her prize-winning Brahman bull. He was a beautiful animal, his dark gray hide sleek and shiny, his huge body built along powerful lines. For the second time in a week he'd knocked down a stretch of fence so he could go courting the neighbor "ladies." Now he stood on the side of the road, a mile from home, all but ignoring her as he stared wistfully at the cows on the other side of the electric fence that marked the boundary of Joe Pearson's ranch.

"This is not a good day to play Casanova," she scolded. "The storm's coming and I've got to get to the store to get supplies before the roads ice up. Now why don't you be a good boy and get in the trailer so I can take you home? I've got a nice big bale of hay waiting for you in the barn."

Bubba only lowed longingly for the cows that had turned their backs on him and headed for their own barn.

Swearing under her breath, Rose pulled her coat closer and tried to ignore her freezing feet, the ache in her lower back that never seemed to go away, the tiredness that pulled at her like an undertow. If she could just sit down for a moment... But one look at the stubborn animal beside her told her that wasn't going to be possible.

"All right," she sighed. "Time for a change in strategy. How about a snack, hmm?" Pulling out one of the molasses-flavored treats she always kept in her pocket, she waved it under Bubba's nose temptingly. She almost laughed when he hesitated, clearly torn between the treat and the cows that were just out of reach.

"I know it's a tough choice," she chuckled, "but trust me, you don't want to go through a hot fence to get to those cows."

Bubba, obviously deciding the same thing, turned to follow her as she backed away from him toward where she'd parked her truck and trailer on the other side of the road.

Grinning, she held the treat just out of reach. "You're so easy, sweetheart. C'mon, just a little further. Once you get in the trailer, it's all—"

Suddenly, without warning, a battered pickup thundered around a blind curve in the road and raced toward her and Bubba like a bat out of hell. The treat she held fell unnoticed to the ground. Time froze. She had only an instant to scream, to move, and found to her horror that she could do neither. Paralyzed with shock, every drop of blood drained from her face.

Brakes screamed. In what seemed like slow motion, the truck swerved to a stop at cross angles to the road. Before it shuddered to a stop, the driver was kicking his door open, the heated curses he spit out hanging in the air like blue icicles. Then, while Rose's dazed brain was still registering the fact that she hadn't been hit, the driver stepped out of the truck and her past came marching toward her with long, angry strides.

Sullivan Jones.

Shaking her head in denial, she tried to back up, to run, but a sudden darkness pressed down upon her. She lifted a trembling hand to ward it off, but there was no stopping it. In the next instant everything went black.

"What the hell!" Sullivan jumped toward her, lightning quick as he caught her only seconds before she could hit the cold pavement. Speak of the devil, he thought, tightening his grip on her sagging body. He'd been on his way out to see her, his thoughts on the revenge he had planned for her, when fate had thrown her right in his path. If he hadn't been holding her, he might have enjoyed the irony of the situation. But she was too close, her body too boneless, the memories dredged up by her half-forgotten scent too vivid—the smoothness of her skin under his hands, the heat of her mouth destroying his control, the innocence of her eyes driving him mad.

Suddenly realizing where his thoughts had wandered, he almost snorted in contempt. *Innocence!* Rose Kelly MacDonald hadn't been innocent the day she was born. His father had claimed she was nothing but a little gold digger after the richest bachelor in the county, and the day she had married Frank Mac-Donald, she'd proved him right. If she could marry to get a ranch, why couldn't he? It was the ultimate revenge.

Ignoring the feel of her in his arms, he hoisted her closer to his chest and started toward his truck. But he'd only taken two steps when the huge Brahman bull that had been following her across the road like a puppy only moments before snorted warningly. Sullivan stiffened, his eyes trained unwaveringly on the bull, who stood only five feet away. He'd seen bulls as protective as a watchdog and twice as mean. His heart thudding, he backed cautiously away from the animal. "Easy, fella," he crooned soothingly. "I'm just going to put her in my truck and make sure she's okay. There's no need for you to get all bent out of shape. I'm not going to hurt her."

Bubba, unconvinced and wary of strangers, followed him slowly across the road.

Making his way to the truck step by deliberate step, beads of sweat dampening his forehead despite the steadily dropping temperature, Sullivan turned to carefully ease Rose through the open door of his pickup and lay her on the bench seat. Behind him, he sensed rather than saw the bull come to a stop, but Sullivan never took his eyes from Rose's unconscious body.

His green eyes as cold as the approaching storm, he noted dispassionately that she'd changed in the last five years. The pretty, gangly teenager he'd taught to kiss was now a beautiful woman. Oh, she'd never have the kind of face that would stop traffic, but there was something about her that was far more dangerous than high cheekbones and bedroom eyes. She had a delicacy, a vulnerability that called out to a man's protective instincts before he even knew what hit him. Everything about her was soft—her small but tempting mouth, her rosy cheeks and pert nose, her slightly rounded chin, the sooty lashes that hid large, wide-set sapphire eyes a man could drown in.

And beneath all that daintiness, she had a cash register for a heart, he reminded himself bitterly as he reached for the flapping edges of the shapeless man's coat she wore. But before he could pull it closed, the wind caught it and dragged it open. He sucked in a sharp breath. Beneath the coat she wore a loose-fitting, red flannel shirt that did nothing to disguise her very rounded stomach. Dear God, she was pregnant!

He stumbled back, conflicting emotions hitting him from all sides—horror that he'd nearly run her down, relief that she was okay, blind rage as his plans for revenge fizzled into smoke. Damn her, he hadn't counted on this, hadn't even considered it. A baby ruined everything! Rose was the one he had a grudge against, the one who had betrayed him, the one he intended to make pay. But he wanted no part of hurting an innocent child.

So what the hell was he supposed to do now?

Scowling down at her, he captured her wrist. Her pulse was strong and sure beneath his fingers, but her bones were impossibly fragile. His eyes flew to her face, his dark brows knit in a single fierce line above his narrowed eyes. She was too still, too pale, her skin as white as death but for the twin spots of color the cold wind had whipped into her cheeks. Leaning over her, his broad shoulders partially blocking the biting wind that raced in through the open door, he molded his hand to her cheek, patting her gently to nudge her into consciousness. "Come on, Rose, wake up," he growled. But her eyes remained stubbornly closed, her thick lashes dark smudges of color against her pale skin.

Helplessness stole through Sullivan, infuriating him. It wasn't often that he found himself out of his depth, but what he didn't know about pregnant women could fill books. Was it possible to scare a woman into labor? His blood iced with panic at the thought. If she didn't wake up in the next thirty seconds, he was rushing her into town to the hospital!

Weighted down by darkness, Rose returned to consciousness in fits and snatches. The wind keened mournfully, a low, eerie sound that sent goose bumps racing across her skin. When had she found time to lie down? she wondered groggily. It felt so good. On the heels of that thought, she heard a muttered curse. Frowning, she slowly forced her eyes open.

Oh, God, it was really him! He hovered over her like a fierce, avenging warrior, a beat-up black cowboy hat shadowing the well-remembered rugged features of his face. His jade-green eyes were hard enough to cut glass, hot enough to burn, his jaw a wedge of immovable granite. In another lifetime his tender lovemaking had brought tears to her eyes, but there was no softness to him now, no gentleness. His face tight with displeasure, he glared at her just as he had the last time she'd seen him, when he had demanded that she quit seeing Frank. Without giving her a clue as to his own feelings or any mention of the future, he'd arrogantly insisted that she risk her father's wrath for him. She'd tried to reason with him, explaining that there was nothing between her and Frank but a friendship encouraged by her father, but he'd been in no mood to listen. He had stormed out, then left town the next day. With another woman.

Deep inside the chambers of her heart, an old familiar pain throbbed, and suddenly she was aware of how close he was, how intimately his legs pressed against hers as he leaned into the truck. Instinctively she shrank back against the seat, avoiding the unwanted memories his touch stirred. "What are you doing here?"

Her voice was as weak as a kitten's, but his razor-sharp eyes watched her as if he expected her to lash at him like an angry rattler. "I came home to see my father."

She paled at his accusing tone. So he knew. Everything. Guilt washed over her even though she knew in her heart she'd done everything humanly possibly to convince Frank not to take the Lazy J from Travis Jones. She'd known Sullivan would come back one day demanding answers, and now here he was. And from the looks of him, he was fighting mad. How could she blame him? His family had once had the largest land holdings in the county. Now he had nothing.

Her throat as dry as a west Texas dust storm, she swallowed, searching for words that could never make up for the loss that he had suffered. "I'm sorry about your father," she finally managed quietly, pushing herself upright on the seat. "And the ranch. Frank made the loan before I knew anything about it—"

"Why don't you just save the pretty apology?" he jeered. "You got what you wanted. Don't start making excuses at this late date."

She frowned in confusion. "Got what I wanted? What are you talking about?"

Irritation skimmed across his brow at her innocence. Did she actually think he'd fall for the act a second time? he thought furiously. "Isn't it obvious? You went after Frank and landed in clover. Two ranches for the price of one. Not bad."

Like a well-trained parrot, Rose heard herself repeating, "Two ranches for the price of—" before she realized what he was accusing her of. Outrage flashed in her blue eyes like summer lightning. "I didn't *go after* anyone!" she cried. "Don't you dare come back after five years and start throwing accusations at me. You weren't here. You don't know what I went through." *The nights I cried for you. The fear of having no one. The loneliness. The way Frank was always there, playing on my emotions, my fear.*

Suddenly cold, she pulled the folds of her coat close against the mound of her stomach and slammed the door shut on a time in her life she would rather forget. "If you want to blame someone, blame yourself. None of this would have happened if you hadn't run off. Now if you'll excuse me, I've got a loose bull who's going to try busting through Joe Pearson's electric fence if I don't hurry up and get him in the trailer."

With a defiant lift of her chin, she scooted off the seat and pushed past him, leaving Sullivan staring after her incredulously. She was kidding. Wasn't she? "Wait! You can't handle that monster by yourself. You're pregnant, for God's sake!"

"Don't worry, it's not contagious," she retorted, never checking her pace as she headed for Bubba, who was once again standing at the fence.

Gritting his teeth on an oath, Sullivan started after her. Confound the woman, didn't she have any sense? he wondered irritably just as a horn blared right behind him. Coming to an abrupt halt, he scowled at the driver of a white sedan that had just come around the curve and was impatiently waiting for him to move his truck from the middle of the road. "All right, all right," he muttered. "Hold your horses."

It only took him a minute to move his truck out of the way, but that was all the time Rose needed to get Bubba into the trailer. Intending to do the chore himself, Sullivan stepped out of his truck just as she lured the bull to the front of the stock trailer. He swore his heart stopped when she began to ease alongside the huge animal so she could get out the back.

In the next heartbeat he was crossing the road in five long strides and furiously telling himself that he was making a mistake getting tangled up with her again. Her pregnancy had caught him flat-footed. She might look like she was the kind of woman who could make a man wish he was a knight in shining armor, but the truth of the matter was, she was nothing but a soft-spoken barracuda in lace.

He reached her side just as she stepped down from the trailer, a concern he didn't want to feel irritating the hell out of him. "Hellfire and damnation!" he thundered. "Don't you have any better sense than to get into a trailer with an animal that size in your condition? He could have crushed you like a grape!"

Unperturbed, Rose leaned down to pick up the trailer's tailgate, which had served as a ramp for the bull. "Oh, Bubba would never hurt me. He's as harmless as a puppy."

"That *puppy* seriously considered charging me when you fainted. Dammit, stop that!" he snapped, jerking the heavy tailgate out of her hands. With an ease that she could only envy, he slammed it into place, glaring at her all the while. "What are you doing out in this kind of weather, anyway? Where are your ranch hands? They should be shot for letting you do this alone!"

Rose stiffened. His concern was a little late. Five years, to be exact. "My hands don't *let* me do anything. They answer to me, not the other way around." She stepped past him and headed for her truck. "And right now they're spread out over the ranch getting ready for the storm. I've got to get to town before it hits."

If she hadn't dismissed him as if he were a cowboy with smelly boots, he would have let her go and forgotten his revenge. But before he had time to think, before he could stop himself, he was striding after her, catching her just as she climbed into the cab of her truck. The minute she started to swing the door shut, he grabbed it. "I heard in town you need a foreman."

Startled, Rose's eyes flew to his. He stood right at her side, his lean, imposing figure crowding yet not touching her, his green eyes boring into hers. Her heart jerked in her breast at his closeness, her pulse pumping as if she'd been running uphill. Suddenly the anger she wanted to cloak herself in had a breathlessness to it that terrified her. Fighting panic, she squared her shoulders and stared him down. "It's common knowledge that all but three of my hands walked out on me. Is that why you tracked me down? You've come to gloat?"

He didn't bat an eye at the contempt in her voice. "No, I want a hell of a lot more than that," he retorted grimly. "I want the job."

Two

Rose's jaw dropped. What kind of game was he playing? She couldn't work with him; she didn't want him anywhere near her! She was just putting the past behind her and learning to take control of her life. She'd thought she was making progress, but she only had to look into his eyes to catch a haunting reflection of the naive, tractable girl she'd been at eighteen. She was still there, lingering somewhere in the shadows of her subconscious, terrified of being alone.

Frank and her father, however, had taught her there were worse things than being alone.

Sullivan saw the denial before she even opened her mouth. He had expected no less. Every time she looked at him she'd be reminded of how she betrayed him and married a man she couldn't have possibly loved just to get her greedy little hands on Frank's money. "Your husband took advantage of a sick old man," he said silkily. "Because of him, I lost my father, my home, *everything*. Don't you think the least you owe me is a job?"

Just that easily, he sent guilt coursing through her.

Don't listen, her heart cried. Think of all the times your father pushed your buttons. And Frank, for God's sake! Remember when you wanted to wait to start a family because you felt your marriage wasn't as strong as it should be? You needed reassurance, but all Frank did was accuse you of being the one with the problem if you didn't even want to have his baby. You foolishly let him convince you a baby would bring you closer together, when all he really wanted was a son to start his dynasty.

Mind games. She wasn't up to them anymore, wanted no part of them. And Sullivan thrived on them. If she had any sense, she would ignore the guilt trip and tell him no.

But she was seven and a half months pregnant. There was no avoiding the fact that soon she wouldn't be able to run the ranch at all, and the three ranch hands who had stuck by her side were hardly management material. Tommy, at nineteen, lacked the experience and maturity for the job, and Slim had a weakness for whiskey. That only left Pop, who should have retired ten years ago. Like it or not, she had to find someone else. Soon.

Which brought her back to Sullivan. Galling though it was, she had to admit that he knew ranching better than most people knew the lines in their hands. It was in his blood, as instinctive as breathing. But could he

accept working as a hired hand on the River Bend
Ranch, which now included land his family had owned
for almost a century?

Answers. She needed dozens of them, some to
questions she knew she wouldn't dare to ask. But the
side of the road was no place to hold an interview.
Casting a quick, measuring glance to the north, she
judged the storm was still an hour or so away before
turning her attention back to Sullivan. "Let's go back
to the house. We need to talk."

But when they returned to the sprawling old ranch
house she'd shared with Frank, the questions she
needed to ask flew right out of her head at the sight of
Sullivan in her living room. She'd never liked the
room's grim colors, the heavy, old-fashioned furniture, the pine paneling that had darkened with age.
But it had been six months since Frank's death, and
she hadn't changed so much as a lamp shade. The
house was and always would be Frank's. Yet Sullivan
walked into it and seemed to make it his.

"Well?"

With nothing more than the single word and the lift
of a dark eyebrow, he took charge of the interview.
Temper flared in the depths of her eyes. If she
expected to have even a ghost of a chance of holding
her own with him, she would have to let him know
right here, right now, that she was the boss.

Struggling for a coolness she was far from feeling,
she motioned to the brown plaid Colonial sofa against
the wall. Only when he was seated did she ease down
to the adjacent wing chair that matched the couch. "I
know you left Kerrville to join the marines," she said

in an emotionless voice that never hinted at the pain his actions had caused her, "but not much more than that. Did you spend all of the last five years in the service?"

"No, I got out after two years," he said flatly, studying her through half-shuttered eyes, searching for signs of the young girl he'd known in the past. But that Rose had never been as sure of herself as this self-contained woman. Endearingly nervous whenever she'd had to take charge, she'd only had to look up at him with her big blue eyes to make him want to slay dragons for her. And all the time she'd been about as helpless as a piranha.

"Since then I've been working different ranches in Montana," he continued, his expression now as un-revealing as hers as he named several of the most famous ranches in the West. "If you want references, you can contact Leander Dawson at the Broken Spoke outside of Butte."

The subtle dig struck home, but she never even batted an eye. It wasn't his expertise with cattle she was worried about. Cursing the heat that climbed in her cheeks, she deliberately brought up the subject of her ex-foreman. "I suppose you heard why I fired Buck Hastings."

What he'd heard was that when Buck had tried to kiss her, he'd wound up face-to-face with the wrong end of a shotgun. It was no more than the old repro-bate deserved, and folks in town were still laughing about it. So why was she bringing this up now? Did she actually think he gave a tinker's damn who she kissed?

He shrugged carelessly. "He made a pass. You objected. What has that got to do with me?"

"Nothing," she snapped, stung by his unconcern. "I only brought it up to make a point. Buck made the mistake of thinking I was a lonely widow in need of a man." In spite of the tight rein she kept on her emotions, she couldn't stop the shiver of revulsion that slithered down her spine at the memory of his hands on her. Agitated, she rose abruptly to her feet. "I wasn't then and I'm not now. If that's the kind of benefit you're looking for in a job, you're wasting your time. I'm not part of the deal."

Any last lingering traces of doubt he had about his plans for her vanished at her words. She thought she'd won the game hands down. He was going to show her it hadn't even begun. "Don't worry, I'm not going to jump you in the middle of the night," he retorted. "All I want is a job." For now. "Do I have it or not?"

She would have given anything to say no, but she had quit running from the realities of life the same day she'd discovered she was pregnant, the same day she'd discovered Frank's real reason for marrying her. Dragging in a bracing breath, she prayed she was doing the right thing. "You have it. You can start immediately."

An hour later the storm pushed through the Hill Country just as Rose headed home from town, her pickup loaded with enough supplies to feed an army for a month. The road was deserted, her truck headlights cutting a path through the gloom as an early darkness settled over the countryside. In the silence of the cab the windshield wipers beat out a steady, reassuring cadence, but she hardly noticed. All her attention was focused on the tinny sound of sleet tap dancing on the hood. The slushy mess had been falling for nearly fifteen minutes and showed no sign of letting up. How long did she have before the bridges iced up?

Her fingers tightened on the wheel at the thought, sweat beading her upper lip as she crawled along at fifteen miles per hour. "Smart, Rose," she jeered out loud, breaking the tense silence. "Nothing like a little negativism to top off a day that's been nothing but one surprise after another. If you want something to worry about, worry about Sullivan and that glint in his eyes when you hired him. If that wasn't satisfaction, then I don't know what is."

She scowled, fighting the uncomfortable feeling that she had been set up. But how? He hadn't made a single move toward her. In fact, once they had agreed on salary, he'd been all business as she'd told him what needed to be done before the storm hit. Even someone who knew him well would have never suspected that he'd been her first lover.

So what was the problem? Before she could come up with an acceptable answer, she started across the first of three bridges she would have to cross before she reached the turnoff to the ranch. Her breath lodged in her throat at the sight of ice already building up on the side of the pavement. Don't panic, she told herself sternly, but it was too late. Her insides were churning like a steam engine. Clamping her fingers on the steering wheel, she tried to bring her thoughts back to the safer topic of Sullivan, reminding herself that he'd done nothing to warrant her suspicions.

Yet.

And that was what worried her.

His cowboy hat pulled down low over his eyes and the collar of his jacket turned up to his chin, Sullivan headed for the house the minute he saw Rose drive into the ranch compound. She'd been gone almost two hours. Two hours, for God's sake! While he was repairing the fence Bubba had knocked down, he'd tried to tell himself that he didn't care if she stayed gone all night, then was incensed when he found himself watching the road for her. Damn her, what did he care if she got caught out in the storm? She was a big girl and it sure as hell wasn't his job to watch over her. Then it started to sleet. That was when he started thinking about murdering her. The woman had no right to make him worry about her!

Reaching the truck only moments after she parked at the rear of the house, he jerked open the vehicle's door, intending to give her a piece of his mind. But even in the near darkness he could see she was hunched over, her forehead resting on the steering wheel, her fingers biting into the wheel until her knuckles were white.

Alarmed, Sullivan stepped between the open door and the cab. "What's wrong? Are you all right?"

Her neck knotted with tension, Rose could only manage to nod as she waited for her galloping heart to slow. For the last half hour the truck had skated over the icing road like a drunken sailor. Even with her eyes

closed, she could still see herself sliding toward the
guardrail of the third bridge, unable to do anything to
help herself. Swallowing the coppery taste of fear, she
whispered, "The last two miles were a real bitch. Give
me a minute."

An image of the twisting turns and climbing grades
that led to the ranch flashed before his eyes. The road
would be coated with ice by now, treacherous. A string
of curses fell from his lips. Sending her a hard stare
that dared her to argue with him, he growled, "You sit
there until you stop shaking. I'll take in the grocer-
ies."

Rose couldn't have offered a word of protest if her
life had depended on it. He made two trips to the
house before she was even able to convince her fingers to let go of the wheel. By that time his hat and
coat were damp from the now heavily falling sleet.
Guilt hit her. He was getting soaked while she sat there
and tried to pull herself together.

"Let me help," she said, and stepped down from the
cab. Turning toward the back of the truck, she never
saw the nearly invisible ice covering the sidewalk that
led to the house. Her foot slipped, and suddenly she
was falling. Horrified, she grabbed at the air as she
started to go down. Oh, God, the baby!

"Dammit to hell!" The curse exploded from Sullivan the second he saw her start to wobble. Within
seconds his hands closed around her, jerking her off
her feet and into his arms.

In the next instant Rose found herself cradled
against his chest, his mouth only inches away from
hers as he bent over her to protect her from the sleet.

Green eyes locked with blue, and the rest of the world faded to black. In the sudden silence, awareness throbbed.

Even through his coat, Sullivan felt the jolt, the burning sensation that seemed to leap between them. Stunned, he told himself that what he felt was nothing more than the aftershock of the scare she'd given him when she'd started to fall. His racing pulse didn't mean he wanted her. He couldn't! All he wanted was what was his.

Dazed, Rose could only stare at him, her heart beating madly. It had been so long since he'd held her. Another lifetime, when first love was sweet and innocent and...

Fleeting, a voice in her head bluntly reminded her. Wake up, Rose! This is the same man who broke your heart, the same turkey who walked out of town and your life without a word.

She stiffened at the thought. What was she doing? "You can put me down now," she said tightly, drawing back as far as his arms would allow. "I can walk."

His green eyes mocking, he continued toward the house without even checking his step. "Oh, really? I hadn't noticed. It seems like every time I turn around, I'm grabbing you before you can hit the ground."

Temper flared in her eyes. "Are you accusing me of deliberately throwing myself into your arms?"

"Considering the fact that I've had to catch you twice in the last three hours, I'd say, yeah, I guess I am." At her gasp of outrage, he grinned and shouldered his way through the back door. "The truth hurts, doesn't it?"

"Your ego is incredible!" she seethed, pushing out of his arms the second he set her on her feet in the kitchen. "You actually think I wanted you to hold me?"

As quick as a hawk snaring its prey, his narrowed eyes trapped hers. She couldn't fool him. Those first few seconds when he'd caught her close against him, she'd felt the pull of attraction, the warmth of memories, as strongly as he had. A blind man couldn't have missed the surprise in her eyes, the flash of hunger as sharp as lightning. "Why not?" he taunted softly. "You did once. Why not again?"

"Because I'm not that stupid now," she threw back. "I'm a big girl. I've learned how to take care of myself." Hearing the pain and bitterness in her voice, she cringed and hurried on, hoping he hadn't noticed. "I don't want a man—*any* man," she stressed. "You were hired to handle the cattle and the ranch, not me. So just keep your hands to yourself and we'll get along fine. Okay?"

Frowning, he studied her in silence, the knowledge that something wasn't quite right plaguing him like a bothersome gnat. There was disillusionment in her eyes and a hurt he didn't want to see. He told himself that whatever problems she'd had during her marriage to Frank were none of his business, but ignoring them wasn't as easy as he'd have liked as he forced a shrug. "Whatever you say, boss lady," he drawled, unconcerned. It was only a matter of time before he proved her wrong, and time was the only thing he had plenty of.

An hour later the other hands came in just as Rose was putting huge bowls of food on the round claw-foot table that dominated one end of the large kitchen. Tommy Lawson, always the first one to arrive, came bounding in like a puppy, tall and gangly and stumbling over his own feet. His dark blond hair wind-whipped and his baby smooth cheeks as red as strawberry ice pops, he sniffed the air and grinned boy-ishly. "I knew it! Chili! I could smell it all the way over at the Jones place. Just what a man needs when it's colder than hell outside."

Pop Kincaid followed him inside and cuffed him on the ear. "That's colder than *H* to you, *boy*," he teased sternly. Barely five foot six, the iron-gray hair on his head nearly as short as the whiskers that grizzled his sharp jaw, he had a good fifty years or more on Tommy and didn't mind letting him know it. "Watch your mouth or you won't be putting nothing in it but your foot."

Returning to the stove for a large pan of corn bread, Rose laughed. "You're going to have a fight on your hands, Pop, if you think you can keep Tommy away from the chili. Where's Slim?"

"Right here." The tall, thin man who stepped through the doorway had the bloodshot eyes and florid complexion of a habitual drinker. Quiet and soft-spoken, with a drawn, angular face, he did his work without complaint and never touched a drop of liquor until after quitting time. Even then, he bothered no one. Rose had never known anyone to call him anything but Slim. "Something sure smells good."

"Chili," she said with a smile. "I thought you might need something to warm you up."

They started to agree, only to suddenly turn their attention to the doorway of her office, which opened directly off the kitchen. She didn't have to glance over her shoulder to know that Sullivan stood there, quietly waiting for an introduction. While she'd cooked supper, he'd closeted himself in the office and started going over the books.

Turning to face him, she said, "Guys, this is Sullivan Jones. The new foreman." She couldn't have surprised them more if she'd announced dinner was going to explode in their faces.

"Foreman?"

"Jones? Did you say Jones?"

"Well, I'll be damned."

Pop scowled at Tommy's comment and growled, "You probably will be if you don't learn to quit cussin' around a lady." Turning back to Sullivan, he studied him shrewdly, then nodded, liking what he saw. "You've got the look of your grandpa, son," he said, offering his hand. "He was a tough old bas—" suddenly realizing that Rose was watching him with a grin, he choked "—buzzard, but no one knew cattle better. I'm Pop Kincaid. These other two outlaws are Tommy Lawson and Slim."

Shaking hands with each of them, Sullivan said, "I don't know how the three of you kept a ranch this size going without more help."

"We worked our . . . tails off," Tommy said, editing his choice of words in midsentence. "But it was worth it to get rid of Buck Hastings."

"The son of a bitch," Pop added flatly, this time making no attempt to call a spade anything but a spade. "You should have shot him, Rose, when you had the chance."

"The worm wasn't worth it," she retorted. "Come on, let's eat before the chili gets cold."

The minute they all took their seats and a hasty blessing was said, conversation practically ceased as they dug into the food as if they hadn't eaten in a week. Oversized bowls of chili and Spanish rice were passed around the table, along with corn bread and hot flour tortillas. The only sound was that of forks scraping plates clean. Then they started on seconds.

Only after the first pangs of hunger had been appeased did the talk among the men resume. Horses and cattle were discussed, of course, and then the ranches in Montana when the men learned Sullivan had spent the last three years there. But even as he carried on a detailed discussion with them, he couldn't tear his attention from Rose. She spent more time on her feet going back and forth between the table and stove than she did sitting and eating. She'd only take a few bites at a time before she'd jump up like a jack-in-the-box to pull more corn bread from the oven or refill iced-tea glasses.

Watching her move around the table with an army-size pitcher of tea, Sullivan frowned, disturbed by the sight of her waiting hand and foot on grown men when she was as big as a house with the baby she carried. She'd obviously worked all day, gone grocery shopping, then come home and cooked a huge meal. She had to be dead tired. Why didn't she sit down and let everyone get their own damn tea?

Why the hell do you care, Jones? his conscience taunted him. She's not your wife and it's not your baby she's pregnant with.

Rose, reaching his side, poured him half a glass of tea before she noted his scowl of disapproval. "What's the matter?" she asked in surprise. "You don't want any more tea?"

He blinked, jerking back to attention. What was the matter with him? "No. The tea's fine."

"Then why the frown? It can't be the chili," she added quickly, a smile tugging at one corner of her mouth. "Tommy will tell you I make the best chili in the state."

"That's right," the younger man said between mouthfuls. "The best!"

Sullivan laughed in spite of himself. You couldn't help but like the kid, but dammit, that's all he was—a kid. How had Rose managed to hold the place together for so long with nothing but a kid, an old man and a drunk to help her? He knew the stories going around town—that no one would work for her after the way she fired Hastings—but suddenly he wanted to hear her version of the story. Slanting her a glance, he asked, "Why didn't you hire anyone to replace the hands who left with Hastings? You had to know you couldn't get by with just three men indefinitely."

She shrugged, her eyes on Tommy's glass as she refilled it. "Things have changed since you left. There aren't that many good cowboys in the area now that most of the big ranches are grazing exotic game instead of cattle. And the hands that are available aren't exactly beating a path to my door thanks to the tales Hastings has spread about me," she admitted rue-fully.

"You pulled a gun on the man," Sullivan pointed out dryly. "That's hardly going to win you votes for employer of the month."

"The jerk got no more than he deserved," she re-torted. "Anyone else who tries the same thing is going to find himself looking down the barrel of my shotgun before he can pucker his lips."

The warning was tossed down as carelessly as a gauntlet, and there wasn't a doubt in Sullivan's mind that it was meant for him. The others obviously knew it, too, because they were all grinning like Cheshire cats.

"You don't have to worry about me, Rose, honey," Pop said with a chuckle as he wiped his mouth and pushed back from the table. "These old lips are too old to pucker."

His eyes dancing, Tommy, too, set down his nap-kin and pushed to his feet. "No offense, Rose, but my mama would skin me alive if I fell for an older woman. I promise I'll never lay a lip on you."

Not missing a beat, Slim said, deadpan, "I save all my kisses for my horse."

Her cheeks pink, Rose laughed along with the rest. "You don't know how much better I'll sleep tonight knowing I have nothing to fear from the three of you. Now get out of here and get some sleep," she or-dered, shooing them toward the back door. "Tomorrow's going to be another rough day. And be careful on the way to the bunkhouse. I don't know what I'd do if something happened to one of you."

With much good-natured grumbling and teasing, they straggled out the same way they had straggled in, their gruff good-nights trailing behind them as they hunched their shoulders against the cold wind and disappeared into the icy darkness. Smiling, Rose softly closed the door behind them and turned to find Sullivan still sitting at the table, watching her every move. Her smile faltered, the pounding of her heart setting the silence humming as she suddenly realized that Sullivan was the only one who hadn't claimed he had no intention of kissing her.

He wouldn't.

Even as she tried to deny it, there was something in his eyes—a hunger, a need—that made her palms damp, her throat dry. If her shotgun had been nearby she would have reached for it and tried to convince herself she really would use it. Instead all she could do was move to the table and begin to clear it as if his presence didn't offer the slightest threat to her composure.

The quiet shattered by the plates she stacked, she kept her eyes trained on her task. "You must be wondering where you're going to sleep," she began, then could have died when she glanced up to see him lift a dark brow in amusement. Sending him a withering glare, she said stiffly, "What I meant was that the foreman doesn't sleep in the bunkhouse with the others. One of the benefits of the job is a house of your own. You passed it on your way in today. It's near the ranch entrance."

He remembered the small brick house, but he had no intention of staying there, not when the house that he grew up in was less than a mile away. The only problem was that it was now hers, not his, and he could hardly just demand to move in. Swallowing his pride, he replied, "I'd rather stay in my old home. If you don't mind?"

Rose paled, nearly dropping the stack of plates. Oh, God, she should have seen this coming! Of course he would expect to go home since she obviously wasn't using the house. Bracing herself for an explosion, she reluctantly admitted, "You can't. I rented it out."

"You rented it."

She winced at his dangerously soft response. "I thought it would be better than having it stand empty and deteriorate. And it's not as if I rented it to the Manson gang, you know," she added, defending herself. "The Goodsons are a retired couple from San Antonio who always wanted to live in the Hill Country. They're taking very good care of it."

Sullivan wanted to tell her he didn't care if they were from Mars, they were still strangers living in his home. Only it wasn't his anymore, he reminded himself. It was hers now, just as everything else was that he had once taken for granted. For a while there, during the laughter and easy conversation he'd shared with her and her hands over supper, he'd allowed himself to forget what she was and why he was there. It wasn't a mistake he intended to make again.

His chair scraped the floor as he pushed it back abruptly. "Where's the key?" he demanded coldly, rising to his feet.

He was livid. Guilt-ridden, even though she knew she had no reason to be, Rose tried to explain. Hastily she set down the plates she still held and moved toward him. "Please, Sullivan, I know you're upset—"

"Where's the key?"

Every syllable dripped icicles, daring her to push him further. Without a word she wiped her hands on a dishcloth, then moved to the rack of keys that hung near the back door. Handing him the one to the foreman's house, she said quietly, "It's pretty bare. I've got some things in the attic that I was able to save from your home after Frank took it from your father. I'll get them out tomorrow and bring them down to the foreman's house. That should make it a little homier."

"Those things are yours now, not mine," he retorted. "I don't want them."

"But—"

She might as well have saved her breath. He was gone, slamming the back door behind him.

Stung, Rose watched him leave and told herself she didn't like the man he had become at all. But later as she lay in bed, the movements of the baby keeping her awake, she stared up at the dark ceiling and remembered the way he'd caught her when she'd slipped on the ice. In spite of all her best intentions, her heart hammered faster.

Three

Dawn was just a pale promise on the horizon when the clock on Rose's nightstand screamed like a banshee. Groaning, she slapped at it until she managed to hit the snooze button and silence fell like a shroud. Her body heavy, a dull ache throbbing in her head, she rolled to her back with a tired sigh. The night had seemed endless, the sleep she finally managed to find restless rather than restful. Two more hours, she thought longingly, refusing to open her eyes. If she could just have two more hours of sleep, she might be able to make it through the day. All she had to do was pull the covers over her head and forget the world. Sullivan could handle the ranch—that's what she'd hired him for—and she could rest as her doctor had been pleading for her to do for the last six months.

But outside she could hear the crack of tree limbs weighted with ice swaying in the wind that still whistled around the house. The storm had raged all night, the sleet continuing without letup until an hour ago. She didn't have to look out the window to know that the ice was at least an inch thick. It was going to be a long, arduous day of busted pipes and faucets, frozen gates and water tanks, and hungry cattle. Sullivan would need every available pair of hands to help get things back to normal. With a groan of defeat, she had to literally push her sluggish body out of bed.

When Sullivan stomped into the kitchen ten minutes later, she'd already traded her flannel nightgown for a pair of black maternity pants and a thick black and white sweater and was trying to work up the energy to start breakfast. Clinging to a steaming mug of coffee, she took one look at him and felt her heart jump into overdrive. How did he manage to look so sexy at the crack of dawn? she wondered resentfully. Dressed for the cold in old tan corduroys, a faded red sweatshirt over a black turtleneck, and a beat-up but obviously well-loved bomber jacket, he looked like he'd just walked out of a cigarette ad.

But no model in an ad ever scowled the way he was. Alarmed, she set her cup down. "What's wrong?"

Wrong? he wanted to snap. You're what's wrong! He'd spent the night chasing her in his dreams, all because he'd had to catch her when she'd slipped on that damn ice yesterday. Where was his self-control? He'd known from the beginning, when he'd first come up with the plan to make her fall in love with him again, that he'd never be able to do it without touching her.

But he had to keep his own emotions on a tight leash. She was the one who was supposed to ache, not him!

Thoroughly disgusted with himself, he'd risen an hour ago with the realization that he was going to have to back off a little, at least until he was able to look at her without recalling the feel of her in his arms. He needed space—lots of it—to get his head on straight.

So much for his plans, he thought irritably, trying not to notice the violet circles under her eyes and the tiredness that seemed to weigh her shoulders down. Why wasn't she taking better care of herself? And why the hell did he care?

"Pop's arthritis is acting up," he finally answered, "so we're short-handed. Slim and Tommy are already putting out extra hay at—" *my old ranch.* Grinding his teeth on the three words before they could escape, he continued tightly, "the other ranch. Can you help me here? I need someone to drive the truck while I dump the bales from the back."

No. For a startling moment she was sure the word had just popped out, so strongly did it ring in her ears. No, she didn't want to work with him. She was already too aware of him and the memories she'd thought she had buried long ago. If she made the mistake of spending time with him, getting to know him again, it would only be a matter of time before he invaded her thoughts at will and heated her dreams. And that was the last thing in the world she wanted. Let him wait for the others to return.

But Slim and Tommy already had a full day ahead of them without taking on Pop's work, too, her conscience reminded her. Was it fair to ask that of them just because she didn't want to be alone with Sullivan? What was she afraid of, anyway? She was seven and a half months pregnant, and Sullivan had already hurt her once in this lifetime. She wasn't stupid enough to let that happen again, was she?

She almost cried out that she didn't care about being fair; the only thing she was interested in was protecting herself from Sullivan. Instead she was appalled when she heard herself say, "While you're loading the truck, I'll fill a thermos with coffee. We'll need it by the time we're finished."

At the sight of the truck slowly making its way over the uneven ground of the pasture, the cattle came running, their breath puffing from their nostrils like smoke from steam engines in the crisp, cold air. Bawling like calves, they hardly waited for Sullivan to clip the baling wire from the bales and dump the hay from the back of the pickup before they were tearing into it hungrily.

From her position in the cab, Rose kept one eye on the path ahead of her and the other on the rearview mirror, which gave her a clear view of Sullivan. Slowly driving from one pasture to the next, she watched him repeat the procedure over and over again, hardly straining as he lifted one bale after another. The wind was brutal, the weak sun that rose in the sky offering little heat. Despite the warm coat, ski mask and suede work gloves Sullivan wore, Rose knew he had to be nearly frozen. As soon as the last bale of hay was dropped in the last pasture, she quickly parked and turned the heater to high.

Seconds later an icy blast of air hit her as the passenger door was jerked open and he quickly jumped inside. "Damn!" he cursed, whipping off his ski mask and briskly rubbing his gloved hands over his stinging red cheeks. "If I didn't know better, I'd swear I was in Montana!"

Rose unscrewed the thermos top and poured him a large mug of coffee. "Here. This should help warm you up."

He took it gratefully, for a long moment just letting the steam warm his nearly frozen face. When he finally took a sip of the bracing brew, it almost scalded his tongue. Gasping, he choked, "That's strong enough to melt lead! Where did you learn to make coffee like this?"

Rose grinned. "Pop taught me. Actually he insisted. He said what I called coffee wasn't anything more than colored water and there wasn't any use drinking the stuff if it wasn't thick as tar. Want some more?"

His grin matching hers, he held out his mug. "I hope you brought more than that one thermos. It's going to take at least a gallon just to warm up my feet."

Without a word, she held up another thermos. "When the cook walked out with Buck Hastings and the rest of the hands, I learned real fast that if you're going to cook for cowboys, always make twice as much as you think you'll need and you might have enough. If we run out, we can always run back to the house for more."

Settling more comfortably on the truck's worn seat, they sipped cautiously, taking time to savor the brew now that the first chill had worn off. Silence drifted into the cab, the only sound the droning hum of the heater and their nearly soundless swallows. Outside the sun rose higher in the sky and set aglow the icicles that clung to the barbed-wire fence. Each lost in their own thoughts, neither noticed.

The combined warmth of the heater and coffee soon pulled Rose out of the reflective silence. Suddenly sweating, she tugged off her gloves and reached for the buttons of her coat. Before she could lift her hand to the stocking cap on her head, Sullivan's fingers were there first to ease it off. Startled, her eyes flew to his as her dark loose curls tumbled free.

He was close, though she'd never felt him move, so close she could see her face reflected in the depths of his green eyes. Her heart missed a beat, then picked up its pace, a half-forgotten memory escaping from the dark corner of her mind where she had tried to hide it long ago. Wrapping around her, it tugged her back in time.

Once before they had sat like this in the cold and steamed up the windows of a truck.

He'd nearly forgotten, too. Staring down at her, Sullivan could feel the chill in the air from another February day, the bite of the hunger that had gnawed at him, destroying common sense. He'd reached for her then because he hadn't been able to stop himself, because nothing could have stood in the way of his need for her—not her innocence, not his experience, not the warnings of his father that she was only using him to bait a bigger fish.

But he wasn't twenty-six anymore, and she no longer had the power to tie him in knots. He wanted, *needed,* to believe he'd moved to help her with her hat and coat because he was deliberately trying to make her aware of him, to see if he could set her heart pounding with nothing more than the touch of his fingers in her hair.

But the lie just wouldn't wash. His eyes locked with hers and there was no denying that his move had been an instinctive one. He wanted his hands on her, just as he had when she was eighteen and he should have known better. Telling himself he was giving into it only because it would further his own cause, he brought his fingers to her cheek and slowly traced the faint flush that bloomed there.

Liquid heat cascaded through Rose, pulling her under, stunning her with its strength. *Move.* The silent command drifted through her like smoke from a fire that was just starting to flare, warning her to get out of the truck before she was singed. But the flames were already licking at her, melting her bones until it took all her strength not to melt into his arms.

In growing desperation she clutched at the past and dragged it between them like a shield. "Why did you leave the way you did?" she whispered, shattering the expectant silence.

His hand fell from her face as if he was the one who had been burned, leaving her as cold as the chill that suddenly spilled into his eyes. He made no other attempt to move away from her, yet her question had managed to create a chasm between them.

For a moment she didn't think he was going to answer her. He stared out the windshield, his rugged face as expressionless as stone. "The old man was drinking," he finally stated unemotionally. "So what else was new? He didn't care about anything or anyone as long as he could drink himself into oblivion. Usually I ignored it, but that day he'd sold three of our best bulls to restock the wine cellar. I knew I should have waited until he sobered up to talk to him, but I was looking for a fight before I even found out about the damn bulls."

Glancing over at her, his accusing look reminded her that that was the same day he had argued with her about her friendship with Frank. "We lit into each other, and when it was over, I no longer had a home. There didn't seem to be any reason to stick around, so I went to San Antonio and joined the marines."

"Without even saying goodbye?" she asked, her words ringing with the hurt she'd sworn she wouldn't let him see. "How could you just walk away without even warning me you were leaving? Didn't you think I had a right to know?"

He shrugged, refusing to believe the pain he heard in her voice could have possibly been caused by him. If he'd hurt her, it had only been her pride. "You made your choice. What more was there to say?"

"Choice?" she echoed, confused. "What choice? Don't you remember? I refused to make a choice. That's why you were so mad."

"You made a choice when you refused to choose," he said coldly. "By not choosing me, you chose him."

Oh, she wanted to shake him! "I refused to make a choice because there wasn't any choice to make. At that time Frank and I were just friends."

"So when did you become lovers?" he tossed back. "The next day? You were married within six weeks of my leaving, so it had to be pretty damn fast." Before she could defend herself with justifications that changed nothing, he effectively ended the discussion by saying, "We'd better get back. The men will be coming in for breakfast soon. While you're cooking, I've got things to do in the barn."

Rose glared at him, wanting to argue, but one look at his set face told her she'd have better luck talking to a brick wall. Without another word she put the truck in gear and headed for the house.

He wasn't being fair. All through the busy morning the injustice of his accusation gnawed at Rose, destroying the peace she usually found by working around the house. He blamed her for everything—the loss of his home, his father's death, the end of their romance. Swiping angrily at the plate she was washing, she wondered if he actually thought she could have stopped Frank from taking the ranch once his father reneged on the loan. He would have laughed in her face if she'd even tried. Last in a long line of chauvinists, he had never tolerated her interference in what he considered his business. Surely Sullivan knew that.

Working herself into a fine temper, she noisily finished the last of the dishes, the banging of the pots and pans a childish display she couldn't resist. Oh, how she'd like to tell him a thing or two! She knew he was hurting, that the combined loss of both his home and father was a blow no man could take without staggering. But she would not let him foist the blame onto her. She'd spent a lifetime trying to make up to her father for disappointments he himself had caused, learning too late that she couldn't be responsible for anyone's happiness but her own.

And if there was any one person who could be blamed for what had happened, then maybe it was time Sullivan took a good long look at himself. He was the one who had left without a word, then waited too long to come home.

And she was going to tell him just that if he kept pushing her, she decided as she grabbed her coat and headed for the back door, intending to slip outside to check on the newborn calves in the nursing barn. But the minute she stepped through the door, she stopped in her tracks, her eyes on the flagstone walkway that led to the barn. Someone had thoroughly sanded it.

Sullivan.

Any one of the four men could have done it, but somehow she knew he was responsible. With so much work to do because of the storm, the others had grabbed a hurried bite to eat at breakfast, given Sullivan a report on the ice damage they had discovered so far, then rushed back to work. Only Sullivan had taken the time to realize that she intended to check on the calves after breakfast to make sure they'd weathered the storm safely.

And all the time she had been silently railing at him over the breakfast dishes, ready to give him a piece of her mind the next time she saw him, he'd been out in the cold sanding the walkway for her. Her hands clenching into fists in the pockets of her coat, she stared at the thick layer of sand, touched in a way she didn't want to be. Emotions churned in her like a tornado gathering strength, threatening to sweep her away if she didn't find something strong to hang onto. Scared, she told herself she didn't want his kindness, his concern. He couldn't act like he hated her one minute, then take time from all the work that needed to be done to see after her safety. In less than twenty-four hours he'd somehow managed to complicate her life in ways she'd never expected or wanted. It had to stop!

She would ignore him, treat him as impersonally as she would any new employee, she decided as she stomped toward the barn. And that, after all, was all he was—a new employee. She wouldn't let him wander through her mind, stirring up memories she wanted no part of. All she had to do was keep busy.

For a while she almost convinced herself it was working. She spent hours in the barn, fussing over each new calf, cleaning out the stalls, making sure there was plenty of feed and water. But the minute she stepped outside again, the sanded walkway was there to remind her of Sullivan's protective presence in her life.

Against her will, her eyes found the small foreman's house at the bottom of the hill. Almost sitting
on top of the graveled ranch road that led to the highway, it seemed to huddle against the cold, without a
single tree or bush near it to protect it from the wind.
Rose didn't need to see through the bare windows to
know that it was just as cold and stark inside as it was
outside. The walls were bare of pictures, the floors
naked and scarred from years of abuse from booted
feet. What furniture there was, was limited to the ab-
solute necessities—a simple iron bed that had with-
stood the test of time, a dresser with a cracked mirror,
a sagging couch and chair in the living room and a
small chrome table in the kitchen. The appliances—an
old refrigerator, stove and a black and white TV—
were serviceable, nothing more. Frank hadn't believed in spoiling his foreman.

An image of the house Sullivan had grown up in
flashed before Rose, giving her a quick, poignant
glimpse of the past. She'd only seen the Lazy J head-
quarters once, but she had never forgotten it. She'd
expected a showplace, a large, richly furnished man-
sion that would reflect the wealth it had taken the
family generations to achieve. Instead she'd found
herself in a comfortably cluttered home decorated with
family pictures and keepsakes that were more treasured than modern gadgets and opulence. By hap-
penstance rather than design, sturdy antiques had
blended in with more contemporary furnishings to
create an easy, laid-back atmosphere where booted
feet on a coffee table hadn't even raised an eyebrow.
When Rose had compared it with the precise, every-

thing-in-its-place house she had shared with her father, she had felt true envy.

Now, staring at the blank windows of the foreman's house, Rose tried to tell herself that Sullivan had no doubt lived in countless places just like it during the years he'd roamed the West working as a hired hand. No doubt by now he was used to barren rooms devoid of personality or life, and anything else would only get in his way. But she couldn't shake the image of him walking the bare floors, staring at the bare walls, calling a place home that didn't have a single memory to it. He had lost so much. The least she could do was give him what little of his past he had left.

Why? The question dodged her footsteps all the way back to the house despite her best attempt to ignore it. Why was it important to her that he not live in emptiness? His happiness, his well-being, had ceased to be her concern the day he'd left town with another woman. Where he laid his head at night was none of her business, and that was just the way she wanted it. Nothing had changed just because he had come home. She wouldn't let it! But still her feet led her to the attic and the things she had saved for him even when she'd thought she would never see him again.

The dull, nearly useless sun was hovering on the sharp edge of the horizon when Sullivan finally made his way back to the foreman's house. The wind had blown all day, never ceasing its whining moan as the temperature had gradually risen above freezing. Cursing the busted pipes and faucets that hadn't revealed themselves until the ice had begun to melt, he'd rushed from one disaster to another, working bare-handed in the cold for most of the afternoon. Half-frozen, his hands chapped and scraped, his face numb, he ached in every bone in his body. All he could think about was slipping into a hot tub of water and thawing out.

But the first thing he saw when he stepped through the front door was his grandmother's picture hanging on the wall across from him. At the sight of the old woman's familiar mischievous smile, he stood as if turned to stone. Slowly his sharp eyes took a deliberate inventory of the changes in the room, noting the sturdy oak coffee table stretched out in front of the ragged couch. Pain grabbed at his heart. It still bore his grandfather's spur marks. On a newly erected shelf on the wall sat the horse and carriage clock that his great-great-grandmother had brought to Texas in a covered wagon. As a child he'd been fascinated with the way the driver kept track of the seconds with his whip. It was motionless now, waiting.

His jaw clenched on an oath, he felt a slow burn crawl through his stomach, heating his blood. In all the years that he'd been gone, he hadn't allowed himself to think of any of the things he'd left behind him. Now they were here before him, reminding him of everything he had lost. Damn her, why hadn't she listened when he'd told her he wanted nothing from his past? Did she think he wanted her charity?

It was all going back, he thought on a red tide of fury, his long, angry strides quickly taking him to the door of the bedroom. Everything, right down to the nails she had used to erect the shelf for the clock. And if she didn't like it, she could damn well—

The rest of his thought fizzled and died at the sight of Rose at the room's only window, hanging the heavy blue drapes that had once kept the cold north wind out of the bedroom that had been his from the day of his birth. Standing on a rickety chair that looked as if it would collapse beneath the weight of a kitten, she never noticed him as she pulled at the dragging weight of the drapes. The chair, protesting with a moan, swayed precariously.

In the next instant he was at her side. His heart slamming against his ribs, he grabbed her and dragged her down from the chair before she could do anything but gasp. His fingers bit into her arms, the image of her losing her balance and crashing through the window sickening him. "What the hell do you think you're doing?" he thundered, wanting to shake her when he heard the fear that thickened his voice. Dammit, what was she doing to him? "Answer me! What are you doing here?"

Stunned, her head spinning from the way he had swept down upon her like a hawk snatching its prey, she clutched at him. She'd expected his anger. Foolishly she had even thought she was prepared for it. But nothing could have prepared her for the rage that burned in his eyes, scalding her with its heat. Instinct warned her it would take only one wrong word from her to set it blazing out of control.

Her heart jumping in her breast, Rose told herself to put some space between them and try to reason with him. After all, she had a perfectly good reason for being there. But her feet refused to move and suddenly it was difficult to draw a full breath. Tension crackled in the air. "I was just hanging s-some drapes," she began, wincing when she stuttered like a schoolgirl. Lifting her chin, she struggled for a calmness that was just out of her reach. "I thought it would make the house warmer."

"Oh, you did, did you?" His fingers tightened their grip. "While you were at it, did you stop to think what would happen if you fell off that miserable excuse for a chair? You could have gone right through the window—"

"I wasn't going to fall. The chair's stronger than it looks."

It was the wrong thing to say. The last traces of softness in his face hardened into stone. "Oh, yeah?" he mocked. Releasing her as if he couldn't stand to touch her any longer, he turned to the wobbly piece of furniture and put his foot through it as easily as if he was shoving his fist through a paper bag. "You were saying?"

She stared at it aghast, her eyes wide in her pale face when she finally raised her gaze to his. "I didn't realize—"

"Then maybe it's time you did," he retorted. "A pregnant woman's got no business moving furniture or hanging drapes. There are three men on this ranch who would do cartwheels for you and you know it. If you need help, all you have to do is ask one of them for it."

The cold words lashed at her, slicing right through the wall she'd built around her heart the day he had walked out five years ago. If she'd wanted plain speaking, she'd gotten it. He wasn't a man to do cartwheels for any woman, especially her. Hugging herself, she said stiffly, "Everyone already has so much to do, I didn't want to bother them. And I thought I could do this myself."

"Well, you thought wrong." Snatching up the heavy drape she'd dropped when he'd grabbed her off the chair, he wadded it up and shoved it into her arms. "I told you last night that I didn't want your handouts and I meant it. So you can just pack all this stuff back up and cart it up the hill again. I don't want it in my sight."

He turned toward the living room without another word, arrogantly assuming the matter was settled. Rose stood her ground and glared at his retreating back. "No."

The single word stopped him in his tracks. Pivoting on his heel, his glittering green eyes silently dared her to repeat the denial. "I beg your pardon?"

She never even flinched. The young girl who would have once done anything to please him was long gone. "You heard me. *No!* I've kept these things for you for years, but now that you're back, they're your responsibility. If you don't want them, then you can throw them out. But I'm not taking them back." Stepping toward him, she shoved the drape she held at him. "Here. I believe this is yours. I'm going home."

He had to take it; she gave him no other choice. But the minute his fingers closed around the thick material, he tossed it aside and reached for her again as she started around him, the tight rein he held on his tem-

per stretched to the limit. "You're not going anywhere until I reload your truck."

"Oh, no? Watch me!" Jerking free of his touch, she
marched around him and headed for the door.

Sullivan told himself he never would have touched
her if she hadn't given him the smug, superior look of
a queen who was too far above him to be bothered by
his anger. But at the sight of her small half smile,
something in him just seemed to snap. Muttering a
curse, he hauled her against him, frustration eating at
him from the inside out. Without another thought, he
lowered his mouth to hers.

Four

Sullivan tried to convince himself that if he hadn't kissed her, he'd have shaken her until her teeth rattled. For half a heartbeat, he actually believed it. Then he tasted her. Expecting her mouth to be flavored with the spice of anger, he savored instead the hot, wet, subtle sweetness of a need that seemed to surprise her as much as it did him. Like a silently invading fog, it drifted between them, around them, seeping into the senses, destroying thought, dulling memories, seducing.

Alarm bells clanged a warning. *Let her go.* Somewhere in the back of his mind he knew it was a command he'd do well to obey. He'd forgotten how drugging, how maddeningly addictive, kissing her could be. One taste and a man could lose his head completely and fall into his own trap. He had to let her go. Now!

The silent demand, like a shooting star, faded and died as his fingers tunneled into her hair, urging her closer. At the feel of her soft, swollen breasts crushed against his chest, the past faded into oblivion, the future into the shadows. Driven to the edge of reason, he took the kiss deeper with the slow, languid sweep of his tongue.

Dazed, her head spinning, Rose clutched at him as he swept her into the eye of a hurricane. His hands, sure and knowing and oh, so gentle, stroked her back, stealing her breath, turning her bones to water, claiming her. She should have protested—should have, at the very least, tried to push out of his arms. But she couldn't move, couldn't think, couldn't do anything but drown in a pleasure that she had never found with anyone but him.

Lightning in a bottle, that was what he'd stirred up inside her…heat that crackled with electricity, fire that streaked through the darkness of her soul, setting her aglow. She wanted to melt around him, draw him inside her, and forget the world. It had been too long since he'd held her like this, too long since he'd kissed her as if he would never get enough of her. She'd almost forgotten the taste of him, the feel of him. How had she survived the last five years without him?

You had no choice. He was the one who left.

No! She tried to block the thought, to push it out of her head before it could take root like a weed, but it was too late. Sanity returned in a cold rush that left her stiff in his arms, overwhelmed with the horrifying need to cry. Oh, God, she couldn't! With a muffled cry, she wrenched her mouth free of his and pushed out of his arms, hastily turning away before he could see the suspicious moisture already gathering in her eyes. The headache that had been plaguing her all day intensified, picking up the throbbing cadence of her heart.

One second she was coming alive in his arms and the next she was halfway across the room, her back turned to him as if he didn't exist. His blood raging, his breath tearing through his lungs, Sullivan slammed back to earth with a jolt that had curses backing up in his throat. Without thinking, he reached for her.

"Don't touch me!"

She never looked at him, never raised her voice above a whisper. But something in her tone warned him he had pushed her to the edge. Frowning, he let his hand fall to his side and watched in concern as she just seemed to fold in upon herself and wrap her arms tight across her breasts. "Are you all right?"

All right? She would have laughed at the very idea if she hadn't been afraid it would sound more like a sob. Blinking back hot tears, she choked, "Oh, I'm just peachy keen! Why shouldn't I be? Five years ago you left town with another woman without even bothering to warn me, and now you think you can just waltz back into my life like it never happened." The very idea of his arrogance infuriated her. Turning to face him, she sent him an ice-chipped glare that would have frozen a lesser man. "Well, I've got news for you, bub. I'm not the gullible, trusting girl I was back then. You touch me again, I'll fire you on the spot."

There was no doubting her sincerity, but Sullivan hardly heard the threat. His brow knit in confusion, he stared at her as if she had lost her mind. "What woman?"

His innocence almost severed the last threads of Rose's control. How dare he act as if he were lily white when he'd set the whole town talking and broken her heart at one and the same time! "Have you run away with so many women that you've forgotten all their names?" she demanded angrily. "Surely you remember Norma Jean Perkins."

Whatever reaction Rose had been expecting, it wasn't the puzzlement that still clouded his eyes. "Well, of course I remember her," he retorted in growing exasperation. "Her mother was our housekeeper and Norma Jean and I were buddies from the time we were both old enough to walk. Her old man used to beat her." His expression turned hard. "The day I left, I passed her on the outskirts of town. She had a split lip and a black eye, and she was madder than hell. She'd taken all she was going to take. She had a brother in San Antonio who had been begging her to come live with him. I gave her a ride." Looking up from his memories, he frowned. "Don't you remember? I wrote you all about it."

Stunned, she went utterly still. "You wrote me? When?"

So she didn't even remember. His mouth twisted bitterly. "A week after I left. I'm not surprised you don't remember. In the note your father returned with the letter, he said you were going to marry Frank. A man can't expect a woman to remember an old lover when she's planning to wed a new one, can he?''

Stricken, Rose could feel herself coming undone, shattering on the inside like old glass. No! Her father wouldn't have done that to her. He couldn't have. But even as she sank to the side of the bed, struggling for a composure that was beyond her, she knew that he had. ''I don't suppose you still have the letter, do you?'' she whispered. ''I—I'd like to read it again.''

He laughed shortly, a hard, cynical bark of disillusionment. ''No, I didn't exactly consider it a keepsake. I burned it.''

She gasped as if he'd slapped her. ''Why?''

''Because six weeks after I asked you to wait for me, you married Frank,'' he retorted icily. ''Do you think I wanted to be reminded of that?''

Pain squeezed her heart. Oh, God, he'd asked her to wait! And her dear, sweet, *loving* father had known. Yet he'd never said a word. How could he? That would have destroyed all his plans. She would have never let herself think of Frank as anything but a friend if she'd known Sullivan planned to return to her.

A silent cry of agony echoed through her, the taste of regret bitter on her tongue. Nothing would be as it was now if she'd gotten his letter. Nothing! And he blamed her. One look at his set face told her explanations would do her little good at this late date. Even if he believed her about the letter, even if he accepted the fact that they were both victims, it changed nothing. He'd lost everything that had ever mattered to him. To her. And for that, he would never forgive her.

Despair fell on her shoulders like the weight of the world. She had learned to deal with her own hurt and loss, but his was more than she could bear. Fighting tears, she struggled to her feet, her gaze avoiding his as she headed for the door. "I...have to g-go fix supper." She gestured blindly at the drape that was still on the floor where he had dropped it. "If you don't want your things, then throw them out. I won't take them back."

Sullivan made no attempt to stop her—they both needed some time to cool off. It wasn't until he heard the slam of her truck door that he saw her jacket lying on the bed. Swearing, he grabbed it and started after her, but he reached the front door just as she headed up the hill to her house, her pickup tires spitting out a trail of gravel behind her. There was no reason to be worried about her just because she was upset and had rushed off without her coat, he told himself. She was a grown woman. She could take care of herself. But he still didn't move from the doorway until he saw her park at the side of her house and hurry inside.

The hands rushed in for supper just as they did every night, nearly knocking each other over to get to the table. Usually Rose laughed at their antics, but tonight they couldn't even drag a whisper of a smile out of her. Pale and drawn, her head throbbing, she answered their cheerful greetings in monosyllables and turned to the stove to dish up the food.

Taking his usual seat at the table, Pop shot her a worried look. "You feeling all right?"

She'd never felt worse, but she only nodded, her eyes on the green beans she was pouring into a large bowl. "Fine."

He snorted, unconvinced. "Any unexpected problems crop up today?"

Tears stung her eyes at that, but she hastily blinked them away. "No," she said huskily. "Nothing."

Shrugging in defeat, he gave Tommy a look that clearly said, *your turn.* But before the younger man could work up the nerve to ask her if all the calves in the nursing barn made it through the night, the back door swung open and Sullivan walked in carrying Rose's jacket. Silence, like a dead weight, dropped into the room.

Rose kept her gaze stubbornly trained on the green beans. She'd known it was him the minute he stepped through the door. She could feel the touch of his eyes as strongly as she felt the sudden skip of her heart. Without a word she began carrying the food to the table.

The tension thickened. Every male eye in the room, dark with sudden suspicion, immediately turned to Sullivan. Ignoring them, he told Rose, "I brought your jacket. You forgot it."

She had no choice but to take it, her whispered "Thanks" little more than a murmur. Avoiding his gaze, she moved to the coatrack while he took the seat directly across from hers at the table. When she turned to find all four men waiting for her, watching her, she knew she couldn't sit there and pretend that nothing had changed. Moving to the stove for the last bowl of vegetables, she carried it to the table. "That should be all you need," she said quietly. "I'm not hungry so I think I'll go to bed. It's been a long day. Good night."

"Bed?"

"But it's not even seven o'clock!"

"Don't you even want your share of dessert?"

She only shook her head and turned down the hall to her room, leaving a stunned silence in her wake. Seconds later her bedroom door whispered shut.

Sullivan stared at the empty hallway, his green eyes brittle with resentment. She'd looked right through him as if the kiss they'd shared had never happened. He wished to God it had been that forgettable, but he knew better. He'd held her in his arms, tasted the surprise on her tongue, the unexpected yearning she'd tried so desperately to conceal. Whether she wanted to admit it or not, she'd wanted him.

And he had ached for her. Still ached for her.

He wanted to deny it; he wanted to throw something. But the frustration burning deep in his gut called for a different kind of release. With deliberate care he dredged up every grudge he had against her, every wrong she'd done him. She had a hell of a nerve accusing him of running away with Norma Jean when all the while she'd been planning to marry Frank. Talk about a selective memory! Over the years she'd made him out to be the bad guy in this, the one who had left her high and dry, conveniently forgetting that he'd poured his heart out to her in a letter she hadn't even bothered to answer herself. He'd all but proposed to her, and she'd left it to her father to tell him no.

How the old man must have relished that! He'd always hated his guts. He'd have done anything to keep him away from his precious daughter.

Including intercepting her mail?

The thought stopped him cold. Was it possible she hadn't even gotten his letter? That Lawrence Kelly had seen his chance to finally come between them permanently and had done it without even batting an eye? Could he have treated his own daughter that cruelly?

Yes. His greed would have found a way for him to justify his every move.

Sick with realization, Sullivan didn't even notice that the others were just as silent as he until Pop shifted in his chair and grumbled, "I don't like it."

Slim lifted a brow in surprise, his gaze shifting to the table full of food. "I thought you liked meat loaf."

"Not that," the older man retorted, jerking his head toward Rose's closed bedroom door. "Something ain't right. It ain't like Rose to miss a meal. You know how careful she is to eat all her vegetables and drink plenty of milk."

"Maybe she's just tired," Tommy suggested. "Don't pregnant women get tired real easy?"

"She's been tired before but that didn't keep her from eating," Pop reminded him. "Somebody should check on her and see if she's okay. It wouldn't hurt to take her a tray, neither. She's not doing her or the baby any good by not eating."

Sullivan didn't know how they all voted without saying a word, but suddenly all eyes were on him. "Looks like you're elected," Pop drawled. "Don't forget the ketchup. She eats it on everything."

For what seemed like an eternity, Rose leaned against her bedroom door without moving a muscle, her eyes closed against the too bright light that shone from the lamp on her nightstand. Exhaustion pulled at her, the kind that dulled the senses and weighted the limbs and made every move an effort. Releasing her breath in a tired sigh, she wished she could just stand there for a while, propping up the door, her mind a complete blank. But behind her closed lids the events of the afternoon played like a rerun on TV, the images hauntingly clear and painful. Sullivan kissing her, touching emotions in her that she'd have given anything to believe were long dead. A letter she had never received, a betrayal by her father she'd never suspected. With that one simple act of interference, he had destroyed forever what might have been.

Pain clawed at her, ripping what was left of her heart into shreds. Forcing back the sob that threatened to strangle her, she gathered her strength and pushed herself away from the door. She couldn't do this to herself. She couldn't torture herself with the past and all its mistakes. Yesterday was gone, and she had to think of tomorrow. Of the baby. Nothing else mattered.

Sniffing back tears, she pulled her nightgown from her dresser and turned toward the bed, her body trembling with fatigue. Sleep, she thought numbly, dropping down to the side of the bed to pull off her boots. She just needed sleep. Everything would look better in the morning.

But when she leaned over to work the scuffed leather boot off her left foot, her protruding stomach severely restricted her reach. Her fingers closed around the heel, but she couldn't get any leverage. Frowning, she tugged again. Then again. But she was already tired, her strength nonexistent. Time after time her fingers slipped harmlessly off the worn-down heel, not even budging the snug-fitting boot. Trembling with exhaustion, she was finally forced to face facts. She was too fat to get her boots off.

On a day that had been nothing but one disaster after another, that was the last straw. Her shoulders slumped in defeat, her misery complete. Hot tears filled her eyes and spilled over her dark lashes to flow unchecked down her pale cheeks.

She never knew how long she sat there in silence, her control shattered, hugging herself and feeling nothing. There must have been a tap at her door, but she never heard it until it was repeated and Sullivan called out in concern, "Rose, are you okay? I brought you something to eat."

She stiffened, her eyes swiveling to the door in horror. She wasn't surprised that someone had come to check on her—ever since she'd discovered she was pregnant, Pop and the others had fussed over her like concerned uncles—but why had they sent Sullivan to look in on her? He was the last person she wanted to see now. She was too vulnerable, too hurt, her emotions all topsy-turvy. Maybe later, when she had come to grips with the events of the afternoon, she would be able to deal with him. But not now.

Quickly rising to her feet, she hastily wiped her cheeks and smoothed her hair as if he could see through the closed door. Irritated, she forced back the tears still clogging her throat and choked, "I'm not hungry. Please, just go away and let me get some sleep."

Out in the hall, Sullivan scowled at her door and seriously considered taking her at her word. He was still reeling from his suspicions about Lawrence Kelly, and he had some serious thinking to do before he found himself alone with her again. But something in her voice wouldn't let him walk away. He hesitated, listening, and heard only a silence that should have satisfied him. It didn't. With a muttered curse, he held the tray he'd brought her with one hand and reached for the doorknob with the other. He knew he was acting like a mother hen, but he had to see for himself that she was okay.

He expected to find her standing right on the other side of the door, ready to slam it in his face the minute he pushed it open. Instead she was halfway across the room near her bed, poised there like a deer caught in the beam of headlights, longing to run. Still dressed in the black maternity pants and bulky black and white sweater she'd worn all day, she glared defiantly back at him, her blue eyes drowning in tears.

Stunned, Sullivan felt something he wouldn't put a name to clutch his heart. Her emotions had always been close to the surface, anger and joy, disappointment and laughter, chasing themselves across her face as her moods changed. He'd seen her so mad her eyes had sparked fire, so anxious to please her father he'd wanted to shake her. But he'd never seen her in tears. Whatever crying she'd done in the past, she'd done alone.

He knew he should give her that privacy now, leave her alone with her pain and forget he'd ever seen a helpless side of her. But her tears drew him to her in a way he couldn't fathom and damn sure didn't like. Before he could stop himself, he stepped inside her bedroom and nudged the door shut with his foot. "What's wrong?"

Everything. The word hovered on her tongue and almost escaped before she snatched it back. "Nothing," she said quickly, too quickly. Her nerves suddenly strung tight, she jerkily lifted her hand to her cheek to wipe back an errant tear. "I'm just tired, okay? It goes with the territory. All I need is a good night's sleep and I'll be good as new. So if you don't mind—"

Without a word he crossed to her nightstand and set down the tray of fruit and cheese he'd brought her. When he turned to face her, he was only two steps away. Up close her eyes were shadowed with secret hurts, the strength with which she usually faced him brittle and fragile. Only sheer, unyielding stubbornness kept her on her feet before him.

His fingers curled into fists to keep from reaching for her. "Are you going to tell me what's wrong or do I have to guess?" he growled softly.

"I told you—"

"You told me nothing."

"It's none of your business. *I'm* none of your business."

"So I'm making you my business," he countered. Holding her captive with his eyes, he stepped closer. "Tell me, Rosie."

The nickname, half-forgotten and never used by anyone but Sullivan, whispered over her like the softest of caresses, touching her heart. Sweet memories flooded her, weakening her, freeing the tears that had all but dried up. Blinking them back, she tried to protest, but the words just wouldn't come. Helplessly she gazed up at him and could only murmur thickly, "That isn't fair."

"I never promised to play fair." His eyes piercing hers, he slowly traced a loose ebony curl that twirled around her ear. At the first catch of her breath, his fingers stilled, cupping her cheek. "Tell me what's wrong."

She could have resisted the quiet command in his voice, the urging in his watchful eyes. But she'd never been able to summon much resistance to his touch. With his fingers alone he could draw her very heart from her. "It's stupid," she whispered, heat spreading from his hand to her cheeks. "I . . . I can't get my boots off. I'm t-too f-fat."

Sullivan *almost* laughed. She couldn't be serious! Of course she was fat, but she was supposed to be. She was nearly eight months pregnant! But one look at her anxious blue eyes turned trustingly up to his told him not only was she serious, she was waiting for him to reassure her that her weight was perfect.

Just that quickly the laughter died in him. He couldn't hurt her. The realization hit him from out of the blue, surprising him, but he had no time to question it. Silently he stepped back from her and deliberately ran his gaze over her.

He'd never taken the time to study a pregnant woman before, never had the opportunity of watching a woman's body change and adapt to the baby she carried inside. Fascinated in spite of himself, he compared the Rose before him with the one he'd known in the past. She had gained about twenty-five pounds, and most of it was right out front, adding curves to her figure that had never been there before. Even then, the slender waist that he'd once circled with his hands was only slightly thicker at the sides. Where she had once been as slender as a willow, she was now gently rounded, her breasts enticingly fuller. Staring at them, watching the way her sweater lovingly clung to her, his hands itched to hold her, to feel the weight of her in his palms.

Heat streaked through him, pooling in his loins, hardening him. Stiffening, he lifted his eyes abruptly and found hers waiting for him. "Of course you're not fat. You're just a little . . . plump."

It was clearly the wrong thing to say. Her blue eyes filled like a cresting river. "I'm as fat as a beached whale and you know it!" she wailed. "I can't even see my feet anymore!"

Flustered, Sullivan stared at her helplessly. What had he said? "Honey, you're not as fat as a beached whale—"

Too upset to even hear the endearment, she cried, "But I'm fat, right? You said I was fat!"

"I did not! I said . . ." he floundered, clearly out of his depth. Hell, what had he said? He'd only been trying to reassure her and she was acting as if he had insulted her! Were all women this touchy when they were pregnant? "I said *plump*," he stressed. "Plump as a chicken, okay?" he pleaded. "Pleasingly plump. *Beautifully* plump. The kind of soft, rounded plump that makes a man ache to hold you. Okay?"

She went stock-still, her eyes wide, the silence that surrounded them suddenly hushed, waiting. "Do I make you ache?"

It was the sort of question a pregnant wife asked her husband, a cry for reassurance that a husband answered with love and tenderness and caring, not words. When Sullivan realized he was only a heartbeat from taking her in his arms and doing just that, he knew he was in trouble. It wasn't supposed to be like this! Touching her, consoling her, making her want him, were supposed to be deliberate acts on his part, not involuntary urges that continually surprised him. Like a man with weights on his feet, he could feel himself sinking fast into an intimacy he wanted no part of. If he had any brains, he'd run like mad while he still could.

But she was still in tears, waiting for an answer he didn't want to give. How could he walk away and leave her like that, knowing it would devastate her? Sighing in defeat, he growled, "Yeah, you make me ache." He'd be damned if he'd tell her how much, but the rasp of his voice told her everything she wanted to know. Fighting the urge to run, he placed his hands on her shoulders, turned her back to the bed, and gently pushed down. "Sit down so I can take your boots off. Unless you're planning to sleep in them tonight."

His less than subtle teasing attempt to destroy the tension pulsing between them fell flat. Her heart galloping, Rose sank down to the edge of the bed and leaned back on her elbows. Never taking her drenched eyes from his, she stuck out her left foot.

His mouth cottony dry, Sullivan knew he had to get on with it, then get out of there while he still could. But it was a long moment before he swung his leg over hers and turned his back to her, straddling her leg. Cupping the heel of her boot, he glared at his unsteady fingers and said tightly, "Gimme a push."

Rose hesitated, her eyes on the slim lines of his jeans-clad backside. "Can't you just pull them off?"

"No, they're too tight." Glancing over his shoulder, he glowered at her impatiently. "Come on, Rose, I haven't got all night. Just put your other foot against my butt and push."

The last of her tears dried up at his tone. If she hadn't known better, she would have sworn that he'd never admitted to aching for her only moments before. Placing her foot firmly against his butt, she pushed. Seconds later her left foot slid free of her boot.

When Sullivan immediately turned his attention to the right boot, she sent up a silent prayer of thanksgiving for his brusqueness. She was, she realized, too vulnerable to handle anything else from him tonight. She needed to be held in the dark, her fears soothed, but giving in to those needs could be nothing but a mistake. He may have admitted to aching for her, but she couldn't allow herself to forget that he had every reason to hate her and probably did. And sooner or later that hate would destroy whatever desire he still had for her.

Seconds later her right foot slid free of both the boot and his touch. She felt the loss immediately. Cursing the heat that climbed into her cheeks, she struggled to sit upright, but made no attempt to stand. He was still too close, his green eyes too knowing. Grabbing the nightgown she'd draped over the end of the bed, she hugged it and prayed he wouldn't know she needed to fill her arms with something.

"Thanks," she said gruffly. "From now on, I'll wear my loafers."

So she didn't want him to have another excuse to touch her. He scowled, wondering what she would say if he told her he no longer seemed to need an excuse where she was concerned. His hands had a will of their own when she came within touching distance. And there didn't seem to be a damn thing he could do about it, except avoid situations like this until he had a better handle on his control.

"Then you won't need my help anymore," he retorted. "Good." Turning on his heel, he headed for the door without another word, obviously anxious to leave.

Could she have stopped him with a single word? The thought worried her long after he had walked out, not because of the answer, but because of her need to ask the question in the first place. What was happening to her? What had happened to the Rose who had sworn after Frank's death that she would never again let herself be put in a position where she could be hurt by a man?

Five

Her sleep that night was troubled, filled with shadowy images that prodded and poked and picked at her until she was thoroughly miserable. Her head tossing fitfully on her hot pillow, she knew she had only to wake up to escape the demons tormenting her, but she couldn't manage to open her eyes. Hours passed, the covers tangled around her, strangling her. Moaning, she pushed and kicked at them, but her arms and legs felt as if they were weighted down with lead. Then the alarm shrilled promptly at five.

You have to get up and make breakfast. The guys will be hungry. They're counting on you to have a hot meal ready for them.

The softly whispered words drummed in her head like a tom-tom, nudging her to wake up, nagging her, pricking her conscience with guilt until she finally rolled out of bed with a weary groan. Every muscle in her body cried out in protest. Moving stiffly, she struggled into her pink chenille robe, a frown quilting her brow as the tie belt kept slipping from her clumsy fingers. Silly thing, she thought hazily. What was wrong with it? Concentrating fiercely, she tried to tie it again, but the thick material just wouldn't cooperate. Exhausted, she let it fall from the belt loops. It was too hot to wrap it shut anyway, she decided blearily, and trudged through the darkened house to the kitchen.

Her mind on automatic pilot, she flipped the light on over the sink and carried potatoes and a knife to the table. Plopping down into a chair, she stared down blankly at the five-pound bag of potatoes in front of her and tried to remember what she was supposed to be doing. But suddenly the heat that surrounded her seemed to be coming from inside, making her dizzy. Swaying, she slammed her eyes shut when the room began to whirl, but it didn't help. With a weak groan, she pushed the potatoes out of the way and let her spinning head drop to the table.

She wasn't taking care of herself. His razor lifted halfway to his jaw, Sullivan stared at his lathered face in the mirror and almost snarled a curse at the worry that had been aggravating him all night, destroying any chance he'd had of sleeping. She had no right to walk through his thoughts as if she owned them, he fumed, dragging the razor down his cheek. If she'd gone to bed without touching the food he'd brought her, that was her business. She was and always would be another man's woman, carrying another man's child. How the hell had he allowed himself to forget that? She didn't need him to watch over her; she never had. Under all that softness that stirred a man's protective instincts was a woman who knew how to get what she wanted. He'd be damned if he was going to let her keep getting in his head this way!

Satisfied, he finished shaving and dressing, then headed up to the main house for breakfast, determined to keep her out of his thoughts for the rest of the day. With all the work he had to do, it shouldn't be too difficult, he decided. There was still damage from the ice storm to be repaired, breeding records to update, paperwork that had been neglected when Rose had been forced to manage the ranch alone. He could barricade himself in her office and fill his head with numbers and not think of her for hours.

But the minute he stepped through the back door all thoughts of avoiding her vanished. The kitchen was in darkness but for the light that burned over the sink, while an unnatural silence hung in the air. Sullivan froze, suddenly chilled. By this time of the morning Rose should have been at the stove cooking, the scent of frying bacon and brewing coffee drawing the men in for breakfast. Something was wrong.

He tried to tell himself she was probably just running a little late and still dressing. But the silence that grated on his nerves was too still. Uneasiness raising the hairs at the nape of his neck, he started across the kitchen toward the hall that led to her bedroom. Two steps later, he saw her. She sat in the shadows that engulfed the table, her head resting on its bare, smooth surface, her nightgown and robe draping her motionless figure. One hand lay on the table in front of her eyes, blocking out the light, the other near the sharp blade of a knife.

Sullivan paled, his heart shocked into stillness for one awful moment before jumping back into a jerky rhythm. Her name a hoarse cry on his lips, he rushed to her side. "Rose! Honey, what is it? What's wrong?"

She never gave any sign that she heard the endearment that fell so easily from his tongue. Her breathing a muffled rasp in the tense silence, she lay unmoving, her complexion a sickly white that was relieved only by the unnaturally bright flags of color that burned in her cheeks. Dropping to his knees, Sullivan carefully laid his hand against her face only to swear at the heat that radiated from her in waves. "My God, you're burning up!"

Panic surged through him. Jumping to his feet, he leaned down to carefully lift her in his arms and cradle her against his chest. Her head lolled against his shoulder, scaring the hell out of him. Was she unconscious or was she just too weak to open her eyes? "Rose? Wake up, sweetheart," he urged huskily. "Look at me!"

In the dark clouds of fevered sleep that engulfed her, Rose could just barely hear his frantic voice calling her. Swimming up through the blackness, she raised her head a fraction and tried to answer, but she was so tired. "Sul-van?" In her mind she called out loudly to him, but his name came out only as a weak whisper. Suddenly scared, she forced open eyelids that seemed heavy with lead to find him worriedly staring down at her. "Whazwrong?" she slurred. "Can't . . . keep eyes . . . open."

"You've got a fever, baby," he said roughly. "Just relax. I'm putting you to bed."

Her brow wrinkled. There was . . . something . . . she had to do. "Breakfast—"

"Will take care of itself," he growled, striding toward the hall. "You couldn't lift an egg if your life depended on it. You should have called me and told me you were sick."

The gentle reprimand fell on deaf ears. When she didn't answer, he looked down and saw that she had slipped back into a hot, restless sleep. His heart twisted in his chest. Tightening his arms around her as if she would somehow slip free, he tried to tell himself that she probably just had a touch of the flu. But her breathing was ragged, her face as pale as death, and he'd never felt so helpless in his life.

The back door opened suddenly. Slim, Tommy and Pop spilled into the dimly lit kitchen just as Sullivan reached the entrance to the hall. At another time he might have been amused at the shock that spread from one face to another, but all his attention was focused on the unconscious woman in his arms. She was so still! "Rose is sick," he threw over his shoulder as he turned back toward her bedroom. "Somebody call a doctor."

The minute he reached her bedroom, he gently set her in the middle of the bed and supported her with one hand while he used the other to tug off her robe. Flinging it out of the way, he eased her down to the pillow and pulled the quilt up to her chin. But within minutes she had kicked it off.

"Hot," she mumbled in her sleep. "It's so hot."

Retrieving the cover, Sullivan dragged it back over her, then sat on the side of the bed so she couldn't toss it aside. "Easy, baby," he soothed as he gently pushed her dark hair back from her stark white face. "You have to stay covered so you won't get chilled." But she never heard him. Locked in a world of heat and pain, she pushed weakly at the heavy comforter.

"How is she?"

He glanced up to find Pop standing in the doorway, his weathered face looking decidedly gray in the weak dawn light creeping through the blinds. "Burning up," he said flatly. "Did you get hold of the doctor?"

He nodded. "Dr. Walker. He's Rose's obstetrician and the only one I could think of who might make a house call. He'll come, but it's going to be awhile. There's a new strand of flu spreading like wildfire through the county, and every doctor in town's snowed under."

Sullivan swore, a short, pithy curse that didn't begin to express the fear rising in his throat. "That's great. Just great!"

"He said to try to bring her fever down and get some fluids in her," the older man continued. "Just tell me what you need and I'll get it."

Sullivan stared down at her white face, the dark, vulnerable circles under her eyes, the swollen belly that protected her baby, and felt his heart constrict painfully. "Orange juice," he croaked without taking his eyes from Rose. "And some cool water and a wash-cloth. I'm going to sponge her down."

During the next few hours he lost track of the number of times he ran a damp washcloth over her face, down her neck, under the dark curls that feathered her nape, then around to the damp patch of skin he'd revealed by unbuttoning her flannel gown to the middle of her chest. As soon as the cloth began to absorb the heat from her body, he cooled it in the bowl of water Pop had brought him and began the process over again.

If she was aware of his ministrations, she didn't show it by so much as a flicker of an eyelash. But her breathing grew smoother, her muscles less tense, her sleep less troubled. With agonizing slowness, she melted into the bedclothes as she finally began to relax.

The fever left her so suddenly Sullivan was caught off guard. One moment he was running the wet cloth over her chest and giving serious consideration to stripping her of her gown to cool the rest of her body, and the next she was shaking like a leaf, a soft moan squeezing from her throat. Alarmed, he snatched the washcloth from her brow, but the chills continued, racing over her shivering body like a cold north wind.

"Pop!" Thundering for the old man, he yanked the quilt up to her neck and quickly tucked it in around her. Her teeth chattered in the tense silence. Leaning over her, his hip brushing hers, Sullivan used his chest and arms to hold the covers close and wrap her in a cocoon of warmth. But her shivering only seemed to increase rather than decrease. Sweat popped out on his own brow at the violence of her chills, the worry he could no longer keep at bay sickening him. If the fever could do this to her, what was it doing to the baby?

"Where the hell is that doctor?" he yelled angrily when the door behind him opened. "Get on the phone again and tell him to get his butt out here—"

"His butt is here," an unfamiliar male voice drawled from the doorway.

Stepping into the room with Pop right behind him, Dr. Andrew Walker moved to the opposite side of the bed with deceptively lazy grace, his eyes meeting Sullivan's for only a second before dropping to Rose. He wasn't a tall man, and with his boyish features he could have passed for a college student. But any doubts Sullivan had about his abilities evaporated as the other man hardly waited for Pop to introduce him before he was taking charge of the sick room. Snapping his bag open, he pulled out his stethoscope and had it at Rose's breast before Sullivan had even shifted out of the way. His face inscrutable, he listened to her heart, then her lungs, then the baby's heartbeat.

His own heart slamming against his ribs, Sullivan watched the stethoscope hover over the mound of Rose's stomach, lingering as if something wasn't quite right. His palms damp, he waited with growing dread for the doctor to tell him the baby was in trouble. Instead the other man glanced up sharply and pinned him with his suddenly hawklike eyes.

"How long has she been like this?" he asked, snapping questions at him. "Did she take anything?

Any medication? Has she complained of any pain or discomfort besides the fever and chills?"

"No, only the fever. As for taking anything, she hasn't even swallowed a sip of juice since I got here."

"What about before you found her? Is there any chance she may have taken a cold medication or even aspirin?"

"She wouldn't have done that," Pop said from the doorway before Sullivan could answer. "She's been real careful not to take anything that might injure the baby."

His eyes on his watch as he took Rose's pulse, the doctor nodded. "Let's just hope that in her fevered state, she knew what she was doing."

Sullivan felt his heart stop at the other man's grim tone. "The baby?" he asked huskily. "Is everything all right with the baby?"

"For now," Dr. Walker replied. Slipping his stethoscope from his ears, he pulled the covers back up over Rose's shivering form and stood, making no attempt to hide his concern as he faced Sullivan and Pop. "I don't want to give her anything unless I absolutely have to, so we're going to try to let this thing run its course. The fever's gone for now, but it'll be back and worse than before."

Letting the warning sink in, he shot them both a hard look as he closed his black bag. "You can't let it rage out of control, or she's going to be in trouble. The next twenty-four to thirty-six hours are going to be rough. You'll have to cool her down and get some liquids in her when she's hot, then warm her up when she's cold. So tell me now if you think you can't handle it. The hospital's already full to the rafters, but I'll find a bed for her even if I have to put a cot in the hall. I'm not taking any chances on her losing the baby.''

Just the thought of that happening was enough to turn Sullivan's chiseled face gray. "I can handle it," he said flatly. "I won't leave her side."

For a long, silent moment the doctor just studied him, as if weighing the strength of his mettle, then finally nodded. "Good. Then I'll leave her in your hands." Pulling out a prescription pad, he wrote down his phone number and handed it to Sullivan. "That's my home phone. Have someone call my office every two hours today to update me on her condition, then again in the morning. If there's any change in her breathing, any sign that she or the baby may be in trouble, I want to know immediately. Don't hesitate to call me at home. Okay?''

"Don't worry," Sullivan assured him. "If she even looks like she's in trouble, you'll hear about it."

There were times over the course of the long day and evening that followed that Sullivan was only a fraction of a second away from reaching for the phone. When the fever held her in its fierce grip, she couldn't seem to stand the touch of anything against her hot skin. She tossed and turned, kicking away even a light sheet while her fingers worried at the flannel gown that covered her. Caught up in her misery, Sullivan reached for the hem, intending to strip it from her body and give her the relief she so desperately craved. But every time he started to ease it up, her hands were there to catch his, her murmured protests, disjointed and frantic, stopping him as nothing else could. For reasons she couldn't explain and he couldn't understand, he could run the damp cloth under her gown and over every square inch of her, but she wouldn't let him see her naked.

Touched by her modesty in ways he never expected, he couldn't bring himself to force the issue when she was as weak as a kitten. Defeated, he left the gown covering her thighs and gently rolled her to her side. Once again he dipped the washcloth in the cool water and wrung it out, then slipped it under her gown. With sure, steady strokes, he swept it over her back and hips, murmuring to her, calming her, before sliding his hand around to her rounded stomach and breasts.

Those were the moments that were most difficult. He tried to keep his touch impersonal, his thoughts trained strictly on the job at hand—cooling her down. But *he* was the one who burned at the feel of her soft, silken skin under his fingers. *He* was the one who found his thoughts clouded with a fever that had nothing to do with the flu.

Lunch and supper came and went with no change in her condition. Pop took over the cooking duties, supplying Sullivan with fresh water and washcloths, as well as every conceivable juice he could think of to tempt Rose. Sullivan didn't have the heart to tell him that the effort was wasted on her—if he was able to get two swallows down her at a time, he considered it a victory. And victories were few and far between. Chills chased after the fever, and in those moments all he could do was pile the covers on her and stretch out next to her on the bed so he could hold her and try to warm her.

When she finally fell into an exhausted sleep around midnight, he almost laid his head next to hers on the pillow and gave in to fatigue. He'd have given a hundred bucks for fifteen uninterrupted minutes of sleep, but he couldn't take the chance. He was so tired he might not hear her if she called for him.

Groaning, he rolled away from her and forced himself into an uncomfortable chair next to the bed. Pop and the others had reluctantly retired to the bunkhouse an hour ago, and the house was silent and deserted. Dragging his eyes from Rose's dark curls spread across the pillow, Sullivan's gaze landed on the book lying on the nightstand. He'd noticed it earlier but had hardly had time to even look at it, let alone read it. Casting a quick glance at Rose to make sure she still slept peacefully, he reached for it and flipped it open.

The first trimester of pregnancy is most critical—
Growling a curse, he almost slammed the book shut then and there. Dammit, he didn't need to know how babies developed in the womb from one month to the next or how pregnancy affected a woman's body. That kind of information was needed by husbands and fathers-to-be, not ex-lovers. In spite of that, however, his fingers refused to put the book down. Calling himself a fool, he turned to the last trimester and started to read.

Two chapters later an image of the baby formed in his head, its sweet, innocent features a fascinating blend of both Rose's and his features. How would he feel if the child she carried was his? If *she* was his? Would he be any more worried about the two of them than he already was?

The thought stunned him, terrified him, infuriated him. Muttering an oath, he banged the book shut and dropped it as if he'd been slapped. Had he lost his mind? This wasn't a game, a fantasy. They weren't two children playing house, pretending they had a make-believe baby. The situation was all too real, and the child she carried was Frank's. He wasn't going to fall into the trap of thinking of it as his.

Trapped in the tide of heat that reclaimed her help-less body, Rose didn't hear him swear as he wrestled with his thoughts. He paced restlessly at the foot of her bed, talking to himself, but it was Frank's voice that echoed inside her head, Frank's voice that haunted her, taunted her.

A son. I want a son to start my dynasty. A son to own everything that was once Sullivan Jones's. You will give me a son!

"No!" Her cry little more than a hoarse whisper, she fought the sheet that covered her, hot tears spill-ing from her tightly squeezed eyes. "You can't use my baby. I won't let you."

"Easy, honey. It's all right. No one's going to use the baby, especially me. It's okay."

The softly spoken voice came to her through the darkness, accompanied by cool, soothing hands sweeping over her, calming her. But she wasn't fooled. Frank couldn't trick her by using Sullivan's voice and pretending nothing was wrong. He wanted her baby! Agitated, she shrank away from the hands on her, her temperature skyrocketing with every frantic beat of her heart. "No! That's a lie. It was always a lie," she sobbed. "You never wanted me, just me. All you could think of was a MacDonald dynasty. Well, I'm not having a dynasty, just a baby. A girl." She hugged the thought to her, her arms wrapping around her belly fiercely, protectively. Half to herself, she muttered, "I'm having a girl. You've got no use for a girl."

Sullivan felt like he'd been kicked in the gut. What the hell was this? he thought with a scowl, rage building in him at the sound of the hurt thickening her voice. Just what exactly had that bastard Frank done to her? Promising himself he would one day find out, he gently smoothed her hair back from her hot face. "It's all right, sweetheart," he soothed quietly. "Everything's going to be just fine. You have a little girl if that's what you want. No one's going to take her from you, I promise."

He never knew how long he sat there, murmuring assurances to her as his hands tenderly worked to draw the fever from her. But for nearly an hour his words fell on deaf ears. Struggling against his hands and calming words, she stubbornly insisted she was having a girl and he couldn't have her. He just let her talk and rewet the washcloth, promising over and over again that everything would be all right.

Gradually the tension drained out of her, taking with it the worry that churned in her. Her mumbled protests turned to sighs, her agitation to peace. Her breathing slowed and deepened until Sullivan was sure she had gone to sleep. With painstaking slowness, he started to ease from the side of the bed, trying not to wake her. But he'd hardly moved at all when her hand reached out to grab his.

Surprised, his gaze flew to hers. Her eyes were swimming in tears, yet lucid as they met his. "I—I never got...your letter," she whispered brokenly. "I thought I'd never see you again."

All his suspicions confirmed, Sullivan could only stare at her and tell himself that the loss of one letter changed nothing. Frank was the man her father had wanted her to marry, and God knows she would have walked on water to please her old man. Even if she'd known he was coming back for her, he doubted she would have ever found the strength to defy Lawrence Kelly. But now he would never know for sure.

Feeling the familiar anger that had simmered in him for five long years weakening, he gently wiped away the tears that spilled from her eyes. "I would have never done that to you," he told her with gruff sincerity. "But none of that matters now. Close your eyes and rest. I'll be right here if you need anything."

She nodded and gave in to the need to close her eyes. Her hand still holding his, she drifted into sleep, his closeness bringing a comfort to her that in her weakened state she never thought to question. He was there, at her side, for as long as she needed him. Nothing else mattered.

Her fever broke hours later. Exhausted, Sullivan just stared blankly at the moisture dotting her face and wearily wondered if he'd forgotten to wring out the washcloth. Too tired to think, he leaned over her in concern and placed his fingers across her damp brow, only to jerk back in surprise. She was cool!

Unable to believe it, he quickly moved his hand to the side of her neck, her arm, the silken smoothness of her back underneath her gown. At the feel of her skin, he almost laughed out loud. She was as cool as a cucumber to his touch, her body drenched in her own sweat!

The grin that started to stretch across his face fell away abruptly as he realized that the sheets and her nightgown were damp and heavy and clinging to her. He couldn't leave her like that, not without taking the chance that she might get even sicker. Somehow he had to find a way to change both her and the bed.

Frowning down at her still form, Sullivan swore at the idea of having to wake her, but there was no other way. Even in the grip of fever, she'd clung to her gown, refusing to let him see her naked. If she woke now and found him stripping her, the fat would be in the fire. And upsetting her now was something he wasn't willing to do.

The first step, however, was to change the sheets. After collecting the necessary linen from the closet in the bathroom, he leaned over her and carefully rolled her to her side. As limp as a rag doll that had lost half its stuffing, she let him place her where he would. Satisfied, he unhooked the corners behind her, then placed a dry, fresh sheet in position. Pulling it tight until it and the damp one were close behind her, he laid a towel on the clean sheet to protect it, then slowly rolled Rose back over. She sighed and settled herself more comfortably as he finished making the bed.

Next came the more difficult part. Sitting on the side of the bed nearest her, his hip only inches from her rounded stomach, he shook her shoulder gently and murmured, "Rose? Wake up, honey. You've got to change gowns."

A fleeting frown whispered across her brow, but she only snuggled deeper into the mattress. "Hmm?"

"Your fever broke, and your gown's damp," he explained, lifting his fingers to the dark curls clinging to the nape of her neck. "You need to change."

But she just shook her head and turned her face into his palm, unconsciously seeking his touch. "Too tired. Later," she promised faintly, drifting back into sleep. "Tonight."

Her sensuous movement went through Sullivan like a heat-seeking missile, shooting straight to his loins. And she didn't even know what she was doing. "Honey, tonight is already here," he said roughly. "And if you don't get out of that wet gown soon, you're going to chance getting pneumonia. C'mon, all you have to do is sit up and lean against me. I'll do the rest."

His coaxing tone tugged at her, penetrating the exhaustion that clouded her mind. Forcing open her weighted lids, she squinted up at him, frowning when his face wavered in and out of focus. "Sullivan?"

"That's right, baby." He flashed her a reassuring grin and slipped his arms around her shoulder. His face only inches from hers, he saw the start of surprise flare in her eyes. "It's okay," he said easily. "I'm just going to sit you up so I can get this gown off of you."

Before she could even think to protest, she was leaning against him and his hands were edging up her gown. "No!"

He stopped cold at her strangled cry and fought to ignore the feel of her in his arms. She was sick, he reminded himself furiously. And another man's woman. Why was he having such a difficult time remembering that?

"C'mon, Rosie, be reasonable," he pleaded gruffly. "The gown's wet and you're sick enough as it is. Let me help you into something warm and dry. I won't take two minutes, I promise."

Her mind foggy, she knew she couldn't afford to get any sicker, not without risking the baby. She had to think of the baby. "The light," she choked. "Turn out the light."

If that was all it took for her to trust him, he would have gladly turned off every light in the county. Without a word, he switched off the bedside lamp. Darkness enveloped them, warm and private and secretive. Somehow it only made the situation worse.

Feeling his senses start to hum, his imagination kick into overdrive, Sullivan croaked, "Okay, lean up a little and lift your arms." Blindly searching for the bottom of the long gown, his fingers encountered the warm bare skin of her thigh instead. He jumped like a virtuous teenager and muttered a terse curse. He'd had dreams of dragging her clothes from her, but not like this! Jerking his hand higher, he grabbed the gown and sighed in relief. In the next instant he whisked it over her head and tossed it aside.

ou may be the winner of the

MILLION DOLLAR GRAND PRIZE!

$1,000,000.00	**MILLION**	$1,000,000.00
	DOLLAR GRAND PRIZE	
	SWEEPSTAKES ENTRY STICKER	
$1,000,000.00		$1,000,000.00

OVER EIGHT THOUSAND OTHER PRIZES	WIN A MUSTANG BONUS PRIZE	WIN THE ALOHA HAWAII VACATION BONUS PRIZE
Guaranteed **FOUR FREE BOOKS** No obligation to buy!	Guaranteed FREE **VICTORIAN PICTURE FRAME** No cost!	Guaranteed *PLUS* A **MYSTERY GIFT** Absolutely free!

E
IBLE,
X THIS
KER TO
EPSTAKES
RY FORM

A
NCE AT
USANDS
THER
ES, ALSO
X THIS
KER TO
RY FORM

ET FREE
KS AND
S, AFFIX
STICKER
WELL!

ITER SILHOUETTE'S BIGGEST SWEEPSTAKES EVER!

ovely Victorian pewter-finish miniature is
ct for displaying a treasured photograph.
t's yours FREE as added thanks for giving our
er Service a try!

Silhouette Reader Service™   Sweepstakes Entry Form

This is your **unique**
Sweepstakes Entry Number: 2D 331298

> This could be your lucky day! If you
> have the winning number, you could be
> the Grand Prize Winner. To be eligible,
> *affix Sweepstakes Entry Sticker here!*
> (SEE RULES IN BACK OF BOOK
> FOR DETAILS)

> If you would like a chance to win the
> $25,000.00 prize, the $10,000.00 prize,
> or one of many $5,000.00, $1,000.00,
> $250.00 or $10.00 prizes . . . plus the
> Mustang and the Hawaiian Vacation,
> *affix Bonus Prize Sticker here!*

> To receive free books and gifts with no
> obligation to buy, as explained on the
> opposite page, *affix the Free Books and
> Gifts Sticker here!*

Please enter me in the sweepstakes and, when the winner is drawn,
tell me if I've won the $1,000,000.00 Grand Prize! Also tell me if
I've won any other prize, including the car and the vacation prize.
Please ship me the free books and gifts I've requested with sticker
above. Entering the Sweepstakes costs me nothing and places me
under no obligation to buy! (If you do not wish to receive free
books and gifts, do not affix the FREE BOOKS and GIFTS sticker.)

225 CIS ACL2

YOUR NAME   PLEASE PRINT

ADDRESS   APT#

CITY   STATE   ZIP

Silhouette "No Risk" Guarantee

- You're not required to buy a single book—ever!
- As a subscriber, you must be completely satisfied or you may cancel at any time by marking "cancel" on your statement or by returning a shipment of books at our cost.
- The free books and gifts you receive are yours to keep.

ALTERNATE MEANS OF ENTRY: Print your name and address on a 3" x 5" piece of plain paper and send to: Silhouette's Wishbook Sweepstakes, 3010 Walden Ave., P.O. Box 1867, Buffalo, N.Y. 14269-1867

In the darkness she was all but hidden from him, save for the nearly invisible paleness of her skin. The shadows that concealed her also intensified his senses, making him all too aware of her closeness, the heat of her, the shallowness of her breathing. His fingers unsteady, he fumbled for the clean gown he had draped over his shoulder. "Here," he said thickly. "Lift your arms again."

Silently she complied, tension crackling between them like firecrackers on the Fourth of July. Feeling his way, he guided her hands into the arms of the gown and let it drop, quickly dragging the warm folds down over her head and shoulders. It should have been a simple procedure, but the backs of his hands and fingers brushed against her naked breasts and belly as he pulled the gown down the rest of the way, her softness burning him alive. His body hard with need, he jumped off the bed and sent up a silent prayer of thanksgiving for the darkness.

Not that she would have noticed if he'd turned on the light, he thought in rueful irritation. His touch hadn't disturbed her in the least. Before he'd even sunk onto the chair next to the bed, she'd slipped back down under the covers and drifted into sleep.

Six

The dream began as a full-blown nightmare. Trapped in a burning forest with no way out, she choked on smoke and panic, and tried to run. But the heat was too intense, her body too tired. Her legs gave way, the crawling flames singeing her nightgown. She started to scream, but suddenly Sullivan was there, calming her fears, holding the fire at bay with nothing more than the stroke of his hands. She could almost hear his voice coming to her through the shadows, reaching out to her, gentling her as he pulled her into a hidden pool of clear, cool water. The heat that racked her body vanished, the heaviness that had seemed to push down upon her chest lifted. The vague, unnamed terrors that haunted her left as quickly as they'd come, and only Sullivan's hands remained, tugging at her gown. She felt his breath at her cheek, his powerful chest as he held her close while he tenderly pulled her damp garment from her and replaced it with a dry one. Touched by his thoughtfulness, she tried to hang on to the moment, to him, but the darkness encroached again and he disappeared into the night.

A dream, she thought sleepily. Sullivan would never show her such loving care anywhere but in a dream. From the moment he'd nearly run her down, he'd made no secret of the fact that he felt nothing but contempt for her. Even when he had kissed her, she'd felt his resentment, his anger, she reminded herself as she slowly stretched and opened her eyes.

Her tired body protested the abrupt movement at the same time her room snapped into focus. Stunned, she stared at the chaos that surrounded her. The nightstand was loaded down with bottles of juices, towels, glasses, even a bowl of water, and washcloths were everywhere—the carpet, the nightstand, even carelessly tossed across the footboard of her antique bed. But how—

Images suddenly played before her mind's eye—her head pounding, her body aching so that she had to literally drag herself out of bed to cook breakfast. The knife she hadn't had the strength to hold. Sullivan's voice coming to her through the haze of pain, telling her she was sick, her fever had broken, her gown was damp and he was going to help her change into a dry one.

The baby! Her hands flew to her stomach, a sob of fear ripping through her, tears filling her eyes. Beneath her palms the baby kicked strongly, as if she were protesting her mother's sudden clench of terror.

A watery laugh bubbled up inside Rose. She was okay. Thank God!

She was still lying that way, her arms protectively wrapped around her stomach, when Sullivan soundlessly opened the door and stepped into her bedroom. His hat pulled low and the collar of his coat turned up to his chin, he stopped short at the sight of her tear-streaked cheeks. When he'd left her to check on the calves in need of attention in the nursing barn, she'd been sound asleep, lost to everything but the rest she so desperately needed. He'd expected her to sleep at least until noon and here it was barely seven and she was already crying.

Last night he would have taken her in his arms and consoled her. Today he stood firmly where he was, a frown darkening his face and concern making his voice husky. "What's wrong? Why are you crying?"

Startled, her heart jumped in her throat at the sight of him standing just inside the doorway. From the shadows cast by his hat, his bloodshot green eyes sharpened on her, pinning her to the bed. Rose felt her pulse scatter and couldn't stop her gaze from roaming over him. Unshaven, his granite jaw darkened with stubble, tiredness carving deep lines in his face, he had the rough, rakish look of a man who had weathered a hard night. There was no softness in his unyielding expression, no glint of tenderness in the flat line of his mouth. Was this really the same man who had touched her in her dreams, whose voice even now she could hear in the distance murmuring reassurances?

But then her eyes met his and held. Intimacy. It was there between them, an invisible force, a subtle knowledge that once achieved could no longer be ignored. It tugged at her like the moon pulls at the tide, crumbling her defenses, coaxing her to forget the past and all the pain he'd once caused her.

"Rose? Did you hear me? What's wrong?"

She glanced up to discover that he had stepped closer. "N-nothing," she stuttered, grimacing as muscles sore from fever tightened as she pushed herself erect. When he made a move to help her, her hands flew out, stopping him. If he touched her just once like he had last night, she'd be lost.

"I'm fine," she lied, avoiding his eyes to take in the disaster area that had once been her room. "This place looks like it was hit by a tornado."

Sullivan's hand fell to his side. "You were a pretty sick puppy—fever, chills, delirium, the whole nine yards."

"Delirium!" she echoed, horrified. "Did I say something I shouldn't have?"

He just shrugged noncommittally. "Not as far as I was concerned. Don't worry about it."

How could she not worry when she didn't even know what she'd said? She eyed him suspiciously. "What did I talk about?"

"Frank. The baby. Me."

Oh, God! "I see," she said carefully. "Anything else?"

He grinned. "Nope, that pretty much covers it."

Rose gritted her teeth, just barely resisting the urge to throw a pillow at him. Oh, how he was enjoying this! "Would you care to elaborate? My memory's pretty fuzzy."

"You want a girl," he said, holding up his fingers and ticking off the important points one by one. "Frank wanted a dynasty. You never got the letter I sent you five years ago. And you still like the feel of my hands on you."

A fiery blush spread across her cheeks like spilled wine on a white tablecloth. "I never said that!" How could she have told him such a thing when she was only just now coming to consciously realize it? "You made that up!"

He green eyes glinted wickedly. "Did I? I thought you didn't remember."

"I don't, but I know I would have never said something like that. Unless it was the fever talking."

He arched a dark, dangerous brow. Suddenly tired of her denials, he eliminated half the distance between them with a single step. "Shall I prove you wrong? It's going to take you a couple of days to get your strength back. A man can do a lot of touching when a woman needs his help just to sit up."

"No!" Her voice rose two octaves, but she didn't care. He wasn't touching her! "You just keep your hands to yourself, Sullivan Jones! The fever's gone so I don't need you hovering over me anymore. I'm not completely helpless, you know."

She didn't have the energy to walk three feet without needing to stop to catch her breath, and they both knew it. But he only mocked softly, "Whatever you say, boss lady. You're in charge. Just holler if you change your mind."

For two days he didn't come anywhere near her. She heard the low rumble of his voice in the kitchen when he came in for meals, but it was Pop who fixed trays for her and sat by her bed while she ate. It was Slim and Tommy who found excuses to drop in on her at odd times of the day and somehow managed to get a smile out of her. But it was Sullivan that she found herself watching the doorway for. It was Sullivan that she unconsciously listened for—his laughter, his footsteps in the hall, his truck driving into the yard.

Even then, she refused to admit that she missed him.

Then on the third day she felt strong enough to go to the table for breakfast. There were three pairs of male hands eager to help her to the table, three pairs of legs ready to jump to grant her slightest wish. But it was the fourth, distant, silent man who stood back from the protective crowd that she wanted at her side. The minute her eyes met his, she could no longer deny the truth. She was in big trouble.

And he knew it. She could see it in his eyes, an awareness, a complacency that came close to bordering on smugness. If he'd have pushed her just once, she would have told him exactly what she thought of him. But the man had the patience of the devil. He never crossed her; he didn't even speak to her unless it was about ranch business, but the message he sent her was clear nonetheless. *You can run but you can't hide.*

Over the next few weeks, as her strength gradually returned, she certainly tried.

Leaving the running of the ranch in his capable hands, she turned her attention to fixing up the nursery. There was wallpaper to choose and contrasting paint for the trim, a handyman to hire to do the actual work and baby furniture to buy. She already had a wonderful antique cradle that she'd bought the week after she'd discovered she was pregnant, but she'd never had time to refinish it until now. After clearing it with her doctor, she armed herself with paint remover, sandpaper and wood stain and retired to the back porch.

For three days she scraped and rubbed and sanded, hardly noticing the tediousness of the work, the ache in her lower back, the tiredness that stiffened her shoulders and knotted the back of her neck. Contentment stole through her like the first rays of the morning sun, warming her all the way to her bones as she pictured her baby lying in the cradle, her little rump in the air, a dreamy smile on her small mouth as she slept. One day the cradle would be handed down to *her* daughter, then to her daughter's daughter, on down the line through time, a symbol of love between mother and child. For that reason alone, it had to be perfect.

When it was finished and carried into the completed nursery by Slim and Tommy, everything was just as Rose had pictured it. Tiny, playful clowns tumbled over each other on the wallpaper, the bright primary colors, as well as the antics of the clowns, adding a festive touch that would catch the baby's eye as she began to acquaint herself with her world. Against one wall the cradle sat empty, waiting, the old mahogany as smooth as satin and as rich as the finest burgundy wine. Across from it stood a mahogany chest that had belonged to Frank's mother, its drawers already half filled with diapers, blankets and gowns that looked impossibly small. By the time the baby arrived, she hoped to have it full.

The room only needed one thing to make it complete. A rocking chair. But not just any one would do. She planned to spend hours in that chair, nursing her baby, loving her, cuddling her close as she softly murmured her hopes and dreams to her. Together they would rock around the world in it, so, like the cradle, it had to be chosen with care.

The morning after she finished the cradle, she started a search of every antique store in the Hill Country, convinced that the perfect rocking chair was just waiting to be found in some little out-of-the-way hole-in-the-wall. The fact that her search also took her away from Sullivan's watchful, infuriatingly patient gaze for long periods at a time only made it all the better. He would never have to know that out of sight did not necessarily mean out of mind. Blast the man, when had he gotten into her head?

Sullivan plucked the note off the refrigerator and scowled at Rose's neat, flowing script.

Sullivan, there's a chicken casserole in the refrigerator for supper. Heat in the microwave at 70% power for 8 minutes or until hot in the middle. Enjoy!

Muttering an oath, he crushed the note in his fist and tossed it into the trash can. For the past three days she'd left early and come home late, always leaving a similar note on the refrigerator to taunt him. Did she think he didn't know what she was doing? She was avoiding him, and in the process, running herself ragged. All because he was getting to her.

He should have felt satisfaction. Revenge was sweet and he should have at least been able to anticipate the taste of it on his tongue. Instead he was worrying himself sick about her and it was all his own fault. He'd lost all his objectivity, all his anger, when he'd taken care of her while she was sick. And he damn sure shouldn't have read that baby book he'd discovered on her nightstand!

Talk about brilliant moves, he thought in disgust as he jerked open the refrigerator and took out the casserole she'd left for supper. There was a lot to be said for ignorance and bliss. A man who didn't know any better wouldn't worry about the effect of paint and varnish fumes on an unborn child. His gut wouldn't knot at the thought of a pregnant woman driving all over the state looking for a rocking chair when she needed to be home with her feet up. And that same unsuspecting fool wouldn't work himself into a state of agitation when his pregnant woman didn't eat enough to keep a baby sparrow alive. He wouldn't lose sleep over whether she was getting enough calcium, or a baby that wasn't even his.

Glaring at the casserole, he shoved it into the microwave and set the timer, but it was Rose he glowered at. Damn her, what was she doing to him? She had him acting like an expectant father! And he didn't like it one little bit. He wouldn't be suckered into acting like a substitute father for Frank MacDonald's kid! He didn't even want kids. He wouldn't do to an innocent child what his father had done to him. And when she got home, he was damn well going to tell her that!

But by the time she finally walked in the door it was after nine, black as coal outside, and he'd spent the last two hours pacing the floor, glancing out the window for her headlights, and swearing. When she strolled in as if she hadn't a care in the world, he wanted to throttle her for driving him crazy with worry. Setting his jaw, he said stiffly, "I saved you a plate. It's on the stove. I've got work to do."

She should have thanked him, then let him go. It was the sensible thing to do, considering the fact that she'd spent the last two weeks avoiding him. But even though he hadn't said anything, she knew he'd been waiting for her, his hard face etched with lines that she could almost mistake for worry. "Thanks for the food," she called after his retreating back. "But I think I'll just wrap it up and put it in the refrigerator for tomorrow. I've had this craving for Mexican food all day—"

He stopped abruptly, his gaze razor sharp as he turned to face her. "Where are you going to get Mexican food this time of night? It's already after nine. All the restaurants in town are closed."

"Mi Tierra's isn't. It's open all night."

"You're going to drive to San Antonio? Tonight? Just for a taco?"

Rose grinned at his incredulous tone. "You don't have to make it sound like I'm going to the moon. It's not that far. I can be there before ten thirty."

Of all the harebrained ideas! "You've been on the road all day. Don't you think it would be better to just eat something here and get some rest instead of spending half the night on the interstate? You can have Mexican food tomorrow."

"But I might not want it tomorrow," she replied simply. "And I do tonight." Heading for her bedroom to change into something more comfortable than the maternity jeans and white smock she'd worn all day, she patted his shoulder in passing. "Don't worry, Sullivan, I know the highway like the back of my hand. I'll be perfectly safe."

"I'm not worried!"

Rose bit back a grin. If he wasn't worried, then she was a bald-headed monkey's uncle! "Good. Then there's nothing more to discuss. As soon as I change into something that isn't covered in road dust, I'll be on my way." Shooting him a serene smile, she walked down the hall to her bedroom.

But Sullivan had no intention of giving up so easily. Ten minutes later, when she opened her door dressed in a free-flowing pink smock dress, her black curls neatly combed, her blue eyes sparkling, he was waiting for her. "You're not driving the highway alone in the middle of the night," he announced in a grim voice that dared her to argue. "I'm going with you."

Rose expected him to ruin the evening with his obvious disapproval. At the very least she'd have bet money that he would continue trying to make her see reason, as if what she was doing was totally *un*reasonable. She was all prepared to defend herself with a perfectly logical argument when he threw a curve by asking her how her day went. There was no hostility in his tone, none of the tension that had made all their conversations for the last two weeks stiff and uncomfortable. In fact he'd sounded almost friendly!

Surprised, she said, "All right."

"Any luck finding a rocking chair?"

"Not yet." Still not sure his interest was genuine, she told him about the type of chair she wanted, and before she knew it they were talking—really talking— for the first time since he'd returned, as if the past, with all its pain, had never happened.

The seventy-five miles between the ranch and San Antonio clicked off with amazing speed. The conversation shifted from the rocking chair to Bubba and his love for the cows on the neighboring ranch to politics and dream cars and Montana winters as they arrived at the restaurant. For the first time in years they laughed together—there in a booth at Mi Tierra's, while mariachis played and the air was filled with music, friendly conversation and the tantalizing scent of fajitas sizzling on a hot plate. Time slipped away, forgotten.

It was after one in the morning when they headed back to the ranch. Silence, comfortable and easy, filled the cab. Relaxed, the warmth from the heater seeping into her feet, Rose sighed in contentment and tried to hang on to the wonder of the evening. But her eyes insisted on closing as they left the city lights far behind. Leaning her head against the passenger door, she promised herself she'd sit up straight in a few minutes and help Sullivan stay awake for the drive home. In the next instant she was asleep.

Taking his eyes from the dark road only long enough to take a quick glance at her, Sullivan frowned at the awkward angle of her head as she slumped against the door. Whipping his gaze back to the highway, instinct had him reaching for her before he even stopped to think. "Come here, honey," he murmured, urging her against him. "Lean against me before you get a crick in your neck."

Without protest, she settled against him, her head nuzzling into the hollow of his shoulder, her soft breath drifting across his neck in a sleepy sigh. Sullivan almost groaned, desire, hot and electric, charging through him until every nerve ending in his body seemed to spark fire.

This is a mistake, Jones, a voice in his head growled. *Let her go. She's too damn easy to hold.*

He heard the command, recognized the truth of it, and ignored it.

He held her all the way to the ranch, his senses throbbing with awareness. By the time he quietly parked in front of her darkened house, he was aching for the taste of her. Common sense warned him to wake her and get her out of the truck before he did something stupid, but it wasn't a night to play it safe. The moon was waning and hung low in a dark, cloudless sky, casting deep, hushed shadows where lovers could hide from the world. Giving in to the need, he gently shifted her in his arms and leaned down to kiss her awake.

Sleepily, Rose felt his breath trail across her lips once, then twice, nudging her toward consciousness. Still groggy, she resisted, her eyes closed in concentration as she waited for the caress to be repeated. She was dreaming, she thought drowsily, her heart slowly starting to pound. He was holding her, tempting her with a promise of a kiss. Sighing his name, she shifted closer, sinking deeper into the illusion.

Again and again his lips brushed hers, caressing, teasing, nibbling, never quite giving her what she wanted. In a dozen silent ways she tried to tell her dream lover that she wanted his mouth hard and hungry on hers, but he only gave her a taste of his tongue, a whisper of heat, the anticipation of passion yet to come. She moaned, need rushing through her veins, and reached for him.

Sullivan knew the exact instant she came fully awake. One minute she was whimpering in her sleep, and the next her searching hands ran into the solid wall of his chest. He felt her start of surprise, felt the soft, boneless weight of her body start to stiffen. Any minute she would be pushing out of his arms, demanding to know what the hell he thought he was doing. He'd been asking himself the same thing for the past five minutes.

But he couldn't let her go. Not yet. Not when his blood was roaring in his ears and his body was tight with desire. Not when he'd spent the last few moments nearly driving himself mad by denying himself a real kiss. With a groan, his mouth settled hotly, possessively over hers.

Startled, she sucked in a deep breath, ready to protest, but with a quick flick of his tongue, he stole the words from her. A shudder racked her, and suddenly it was difficult to breathe, let alone think. The heady, masculine scent of him surrounded her as surely as his arms did, drawing her into a world of white-hot heat and seduction. Passion, too long denied, heated to flash point in a heartbeat.

She could feel herself sinking into him, melting like hot fudge in a blast furnace, and could only gasp, clutching at him, her tongue wildly tangling with his. His hands flew over her, fighting her clothes, tearing at stubborn buttons, nearly ripping them free to reach her. She should have protested, was even gathering the words in her head when his fingers closed around her breast. Her *bare* breast. When had he found the clasp of her bra? She moaned, straining against him as his fingers began an exquisitely thorough exploration of her body, charting every sensitive inch of her breasts, her thickened waist, the spread of her hips, the heat locked between her thighs. And with each touch, each sliding caress, each bold rub of his thumb across her nipple, the need in her coiled tighter.

She had to stop him, stop herself. The thought danced to the frantic thundering of her heart the minute he lifted his mouth from hers, but then he buried his hands in her hair and ran quick, darting, desperate kisses over her face and throat and she was lost. Whimpering, she locked her hands around his wrists and held on for dear life.

Sullivan felt his control unraveling and made no effort to slow the pace. Not tonight. He couldn't stop now, not when he finally had her right where he wanted her. Sweet. How could he have forgotten what she was like when she was caught up in the sweet flames of desire? She could turn a man to cinders with just her kiss alone.

And she was his, all his. He could taste it in the red-hot heat of her response, feel it in the abandoned way she arched into him as he cupped a swollen breast in his hand, hear it in the cry that broke from her parted lips when his teasing fingers gently plucked at her nipple. He could have taken her then and there, in the cab of her truck, and she wouldn't have breathed a whisper of protest.

That thought alone was nearly enough to drive him over the edge. His mouth hungrily latched onto hers, while his hand slid under her dress to the tantalizing, silken smoothness of her inner thigh. Passion roared in his head, need screaming through him. He told himself she couldn't respond to him the way she did unless she felt something for him. He knew her too well—

Before his closed eyes, images from the past flickered hauntingly. A lifetime ago she'd melted in his arms, denied him nothing, made him think he was the only man in the world for her. But she'd walked down the aisle with someone else.

He jerked back abruptly, his breathing harsh and labored in the sudden tense silence. Glaring at her in the darkness, his emerald eyes spearing hers, he said hoarsely, "Why did you do it, dammit? Why did you marry Frank so fast?"

The swift, sudden descent from passion left her reeling. She shook her head in confusion, unable to believe he wanted to talk about Frank now. "What?"

His hands at her upper arms, he just barely resisted the urge to shake her. "Could he set you on fire with just a few kisses? Or did just knowing that you finally had what you'd always wanted make you melt in his arms like a prostitute?"

She gasped, stricken. How could he talk to her like that after what they had just shared? "Damn you, you keep talking about what I'd always wanted, but what I wanted was you!" she cried. Pushing out of his arms, she hastily scooted out of reach across the seat, her fingers trembling as she righted her clothing. "I thought you'd left town with another woman and Frank was the only friend I had. Do you hear me? We were just *friends*."

Hugging herself, her eyes stared starkly into the past. "A month after you left, Dad had a heart attack," she said hollowly. "He was dying, and I was so afraid of being alone. If it hadn't been for Frank, I don't know what I would have done. He was there for me."

And you weren't.

The words were never spoken, but they hung in the air nevertheless. Sullivan wanted to snap back at her that they both knew why Frank had been there, but he held his tongue, a muscle ticking in his jaw. "So if you were just friends," he finally growled, "then how the hell did you end up married to him?"

"When I finally realized that Dad wasn't going to make it, Frank promised to protect me, to take care of me." She swallowed, forcing moisture into her dry throat. "I thought he loved me and he convinced me that I could love him if I just let myself." At Sullivan's snort of disdain, she snapped, "I was eighteen, just a kid, and I needed to believe him. And Dad had always wanted me to marry Frank. He said he could die happy knowing I was taken care of by a man like Frank."

Sullivan's mouth flattened into a hard line. She'd always been a sucker for the guilt trips her old man had laid on her. He could just imagine him putting her through a horrible deathbed scene just to push her into Frank's arms.

Suddenly realizing the direction his thoughts had turned, he brought them to a screeching stop. What the hell was he doing? Making excuses for her? Thinking of her as the innocent in all this? How could she be the innocent when she'd ended up with everything?

"Your dad would have pushed you off on Attila the Hun if he'd thought he had the bucks," he retorted contemptuously, clinging to his anger. "He didn't care about what kind of husband Frank would be, only how much money he had."

He didn't say anything she hadn't thought herself, but somehow knowing that he, too, knew how little value her father had placed on her was more than she could bear. Suddenly she'd had enough. Grabbing up her purse and coat, she searched for the door handle. "Believe what you like," she said coldly. "You will anyway. But if you came back after all these years just for revenge, you wasted your time. I didn't do anything to you, and I'm not going to let you hurt me. Not again. My days of being manipulated by men are over. Just stay away from me." Pushing open the door, she climbed out and slammed it shut, then walked into the dark house alone.

Seven

——

After that, a state of cold war settled over the ranch like a heat wave that showed no sign of breaking. Tension built until the air became so close and dense that even the hands noticed. Smiles faded, then disappeared altogether. Meals became something to be endured, the jokes that were usually passed back and forth across the table turned into stilted conversations that swiftly faded into long, awkward silences. And with each passing day the threat of an explosion grew more imminent.

A black scowl on his face, Sullivan went about his duties growling at anyone who got in his way. He knew the men were cutting him a wide berth, but Rose didn't even bother to avoid him. She simply withdrew into herself. She didn't smile, she didn't talk except when it was absolutely necessary, and her appetite became nonexistent. Worry crept into the frustration eating at him, infuriating him all the more. He found himself wanting to shake her, to demand that she take care of herself, that she quit doing this to him. She was driving him crazy!

How could he carry out his plans when she continued to confound him the way she did? He'd been so sure his revenge was perfectly justified, so sure that nothing she could say would excuse what she had done. The facts had seemed cut and dried, damning. But nothing was turning out as he'd expected. He had underestimated Lawrence Kelly and forgotten what lengths the man would go to get what he wanted—a rich son-in-law. He wouldn't have hesitated to sacrifice his daughter's happiness to achieve his own blind ambition. Now that he'd had time to think about it, Sullivan could hear the pain thickening Rose's voice when she'd told him she wouldn't be manipulated again. A muscle ticked along his jaw. She wasn't supposed to be hurting!

Rose saw the way he watched her when he didn't think she was looking, his frown fierce, the concern darkening his eyes making her want to scream. How dare he act as if he cared about her! He was only out for revenge. That's all he had wanted from her since the day he'd returned. All his kisses, all his gentleness when he'd taken care of her when she was sick, all the worry he'd shown when she pushed herself too hard, was nothing but a ruse to hide his real intent. He was going to make her pay for what he'd lost with a piece of her heart. She had never been so miserable in her life.

Seven nights after their run to San Antonio, Rose stood in the kitchen and stared out at the dark, wet night, hugging herself against her own tortured thoughts and the dampness that seemed to slip beneath the window and crawl into her bones. The rain had started yesterday, sometime during the middle of the night, and was still coming down in buckets. Pop, Slim and Tommy had pulled on slickers after supper and gone out to move the cattle near the river to higher ground, their curses nearly drowned out by the rumble of thunder directly overhead. Watching them disappear into the darkness, Rose silently agreed that it was a lousy night. But what other way could you expect to end a horrible week?

She knew she was in a rotten mood, but there didn't seem to be anything she could do about it. There'd been a constant ache in her back ever since the rain had started; the baby's movements over the last three nights had robbed her of sleep, and every time she turned around, she found herself wanting to cry. She was tired...tired of the waiting, tired of the rain, tired of the heartache that only seemed to deepen every time her eyes collided with Sullivan's.

"We need to discuss the buying trip I'm leaving on next week."

She didn't have to glance over her shoulder to know that he was standing at the doorway to her office watching her watch the rain. Stubbornly she stayed where she was, her hand absently kneading her lower back. "Can't it wait until tomorrow?" She couldn't deal with him tonight, not when they were so cut off from the rest of the world and her nerves were skittish and shaky.

"Why not now?" he insisted. "I've already gone through the marketing tapes and picked out some good stock from several ranches out west. I just need you to look them over and okay what I've selected—"

Rose whirled, sparks flaring in her blue eyes. "What *you've* selected?"

Her sharp tone, as well as her obvious objection, caught him by surprise. Why, after nearly a week of hardly speaking to him, was she snapping his head off now? Feeling his way carefully, he said, "Nothing's carved in stone. I've just pulled some tapes I thought you'd be interested in. I was under the impression that was part of my job."

It was. Twin spots of color burned in her cheeks. How dare he be so reasonable! Of course buying new cattle to improve the herd was part of his job, but he didn't have to act as if it was *his* cattle, *his* ranch, he was improving. He was taking over with frightening ease, making it so easy for her to hand over all responsibility to him, to lean on him as if he would always be there for her. But how long would he stay after he got the revenge he thought he deserved?

"Which ranches do you plan to visit?" she demanded stonily.

His eyes narrowed, but all he said was, "The Broken Arrow in Montana, the Rolling R in Colorado and the Twisted Snake in New Mexico."

"Frank never did business with any of them."

It was the ultimate insult. He stiffened, so tempted to tell her that Frank wouldn't have known good bloodlines from a hole in the ground that he could taste it. But as he opened his mouth to do just that, he caught a glimpse of himself in his memory, sitting by her bed reading about how precarious a woman's emotional state was during pregnancy, especially as she neared her time. Helplessness stole through him, his irritation fizzling. How did any man live through his woman's pregnancy without going stark, staring mad?

Dragging in a steadying breath, he said with a calmness he was proud of, "Then give me a list of the ranchers Frank dealt with and I'll contact them. You're the boss."

She was, but she was beginning to hate having him remind her of it. "I'm not pulling rank—"

"I didn't say you were," he said patiently. "Just tell me what you want me to do, sweetheart, and I'll do it."

She wanted to ask him to hold her, to call her sweetheart again, to assure her that his kisses had had nothing to do with revenge. But she couldn't. Turning back to the window, she wrapped her arms around herself and gazed out at the wet night. "I'm sure the cattle you've chosen will be fine," she said huskily. "Just leave the tapes on the desk and I'll look them over tomorrow. I'm too tired tonight. I'm going to bed early."

It was a clear dismissal, but he hated leaving her when she seemed so upset. Yet if he stayed, he'd have to touch her, and in her present mood she might scratch his eyes out. Reluctantly moving to the coat-rack next to the back door, he pulled on his bright yellow slicker, then tugged his cowboy hat down low over his eyes. "Then I'll get out of your way. See you in the morning."

Rose held herself stiffly, her quiet good-night cut off by the closing of the back door. Seconds later she caught the blurred flash of his headlights in the rain as he turned his truck toward the foreman's house. Only then, when she was sure she was alone, did she allow herself the luxury of tears.

Flat on his back, Sullivan glared at the ceiling over his bed, listening to the rain that drummed against the tin roof. It was no use, he thought in disgust, giving up on the sleep that wouldn't come. He couldn't get Rose out of his head. Every time he closed his eyes she came to him in the darkness, her blue eyes clouded and un-certain, dark with hurt, a trace of fear, a longing she wouldn't admit to. She'd given him just that same look earlier in the kitchen. He'd wanted to hold her then, to take her in his arms and keep her safe through the night, through all the nights to come until she had the baby. A woman in her condition, less than a month away from her time, had no business being alone. She needed a man at her side.

And he, like it or not, needed to be that man.

The truth, refusing to be ignored, shouted at him in the dark stillness that engulfed him. With a sigh of defeat, he dropped his arm over his eyes. What a mess.

* * *

When the phone rang an hour later he was just tee-tering on the edge of sleep. Cocking open one eye, he glowered at the clock on the nightstand. Two o'clock in the morning. Cursing under his breath, he fumbled for the phone and dragged the receiver to his ear. "Yeah?" he mumbled.

"Sullivan?"

At the sound of Rose's tremulous whisper, a sharp, inexplicable fear snaked into his stomach. He bolted upright, his bare feet hitting the floor with a thud. "What is it, honey? What's wrong?"

"It's..." She hesitated, as if her throat suddenly closed up and she couldn't get the words out. He heard her swallow what he thought was a sob. "I...th-think it's t-time."

Confused, he clutched the phone tighter. "Time for what, sweetheart? What's going on?"

"The baby," she choked. "I think the baby's com-ing."

"It can't be," he said stupidly. "It's not due for another month, is it?"

She almost laughed at that as her breath caught on a giggle. "I don't think she cares that she's early. She's com—"

A hiss of surprised pain cut through whatever she was going to say and leapt through the phone to stab Sullivan right in the heart. He paled. "Just sit tight," he ordered hoarsely. "I'll be right there."

He banged the receiver down without waiting for her to answer, then almost tripped over his own feet when he tried to tug on his jeans with fingers that were suddenly all thumbs. Panic, like a thief in the night, slid through his veins. She couldn't be having the baby now! It was too soon! Jamming his feet into his boots without bothering with socks, he snatched up the nearest shirt he could find—a torn T-shirt. He was pulling it over his head when he slammed out the back door into the driving rain.

Five minutes later he rushed into her kitchen like a wild man, his wet hair standing on end, his soaked T-shirt plastered to his chest, a wide hole exposing one hairy underarm. At the sight of Rose calmly pacing the kitchen in a red plaid flannel gown and matching robe, he stopped short, gasping for breath. "Are you okay?" he asked anxiously.

She nodded, her throat suddenly constricted with tears. The sick fear that had gripped her ever since she'd realized she was in labor vanished the minute Sullivan walked in the door, his wet face dark with stubble, his green eyes wide with worry. Peace settled over her. Everything would be okay now. He wouldn't let anything happen to her baby. Resuming her pacing, she shot him a relieved smile. "I'm fine. Just a little nervous. I haven't done this before."

Neither had he, but he sure as hell wasn't fine! Ignoring the water he dripped on the floor, he started toward her nervously. "Sweetheart, you should be in bed. C'mon, I'll help you, then I'll call the doctor."

She turned away. "No, I don't want to go to bed. I need to walk."

Oh, God, she was going to be stubborn, he thought with a groan. He could see it in the set of her jaw. Following behind her, he tried to reason with her.

"You're only going to wear yourself out prowling the kitchen like a caged tiger, honey. Don't you want to lie down? You'll be a lot more comfortable in your own bed."

"No, I won't. The pressure starts to build—" Her words trailed off as she stopped suddenly and reached out to grab the back of a kitchen chair.

From half a room away Sullivan watched her breathing splinter, the soft lines of her face slowly tighten with the contraction that clawed at her with gradually sharpening talons. Her breathing changed, deepened. Inhale. Exhale. He could almost hear the rhythm of her thoughts, almost feel the concentration that helped to partially block out the pain.

Then, suddenly, it was over. She released a final gust of triumph and determinedly resumed her pacing, her heart-shaped face untroubled and free of pain. "I've got to walk."

Shaken, Sullivan couldn't manage a single word of protest. It was *his* gut that still clenched in a contraction, his heart that still wheezed with panic. Suddenly there was no avoiding the truth. In spite of all the times he'd warned himself not to get wrapped up in Frank's baby, he felt as if it was his baby she was having, his baby that was coming into the world a month too early.

He wasn't ready for this.

Panic skipped through him like a rock skipping water, the ripples spreading outward, threatening to swallow him whole. Galvanized into action, he jumped toward the bedroom. "To hell with calling the doctor now. I'll call him from the hospital. Where's your suitcase?''

''In the hall closet. But—''

He didn't wait to hear more. Striding into the hall, he jerked open the closet door and pulled out the overnight case sitting right in the front. The minute he felt its light weight, he glared at her accusingly. ''You haven't packed.''

''I didn't think I needed to for at least another couple of weeks,'' she defended herself. ''How was I supposed to know the baby would come this early?''

''What do you need? Gowns? Underwear? Socks? Anything else?'' Striding into her room, he yanked open drawers and pulled out the items she'd need, haphazardly throwing them into the small case. Seconds later he locked it and headed for the back door. ''Let's go.''

Rose stayed stubbornly where she was, fighting the urge to laugh. He was more nervous than she was! ''Sullivan, there's plenty of time to get to the hospital. My contractions just started. The baby won't be here for hours.''

He hesitated, then slowly turned back to face her, wishing he didn't have to worry her now, when she already had so much on her mind. But she had to know what they were up against. ''The river's been rising for hours, honey. If we don't leave now, we might not be able to make it into town at all.''

Her smile faltered as she reached out to steady herself, feeling as if her knees had just been knocked out from under her. ''I never realized . . . I wasn't thinking . . .''

He was at her side instantly, gently swinging her up into his arms and carrying her to the back door. "Don't start panicking on me now, babe. I promise you everything's going to be fine. You just relax and let me take care of the details."

But everything wasn't fine. Ten minutes later Sullivan braked to a stop on a small rise, the steady beat of the windshield wipers loud in the sudden silence. Together they followed the beam of the headlights to the muddy, raging water rushing over the top of the first of the three bridges that stood between them and town. Without a word, he turned the truck around and headed back to the house.

Another contraction hit Rose the minute she stepped back into the kitchen. Worry clogging her throat, she started gritting her teeth as she fought the pain. She never saw Sullivan come in behind her, never felt him slip his arm around her and pull her against him. But suddenly he was there, his husky murmur in her ear calming her, soothing her, quieting her. "Easy, honey, don't tense up. Breathe through it. Take deep breaths and let them out through your mouth. Slow and easy. That's it. You're doing fine."

With agonizing slowness, the pain lessened, withdrawing like receding floodwaters until it disappeared altogether. Only then did Rose start to tremble. She wasn't going to make it to the hospital. "Sullivan..." She clutched at him, fear eroding her control. "The baby...it's too soon! I need a doctor. How can I have a premature baby without a doctor?"

Unnerved, Sullivan was wondering the same thing, but the last thing she needed now was his doubts. She was already unraveling in his arms. With a confidence that was nothing but pure bluff, he promised, "You'll have your doctor, honey. You said yourself that the baby won't be here for hours. That gives me plenty of time to find a way to get you to the hospital." Tightening his arm around her reassuringly, he led her to her bedroom. "While I'm doing that, I want you to stop panicking and get some rest. You're going to need your strength. Okay?"

She nodded. But as he helped her into bed, she couldn't let him go without voicing her biggest fear. Taking his hand, she held him at her bedside, her eyes searching his. "What do you know about delivering babies?"

"Honey, it's not going to come to that—"

"But what if it does?" she insisted. "I need to know from the outset if we're flying blind here."

He could have lied to her. She was looking for reassurance, not the truth, and at that moment he could have claimed to have delivered a half dozen kids and she never would have questioned him. But when her deep blue eyes gazed up at him so trustingly, he couldn't be anything but honest with her. "Not a heck of a lot," he replied grimly. "I read one of your baby books while you were sick, so I know pretty much what to expect. But if you're asking if I've ever helped deliver a baby, the answer is no."

She swallowed. She'd wanted the truth; she'd gotten it. "Then I guess this is a first time for both of us," she said with a forced lightness that fell miserably flat.

"Hey, don't give up on me so soon," he teased, brushing her hair back from her ashen face. "I may have to call in the National Guard, but I'll find a way to get you out of here in time." Easing his hand from hers, he backed toward the door. "While you're resting, I'm going to make some calls from the kitchen. I'll be back before the next contraction starts."

He was as good as his word. Her eyes closed, all her concentration focused on her breathing as the tension slowly started to tighten in her abdomen, she didn't realize he was there until his hand closed over her fingers where they gripped the sheet. Through the gradually darkening red haze of pain that shrouded her, she heard him whisper, "That a girl. You're doing great. Dr. Walker's going to have a helicopter here at dawn to take you to the hospital." His fingers squeezed hers. "You hear me, sweetheart? You just hang in there a couple more hours, and the baby will be born at Kerrville General just as you planned. Everything's going to be fine. Just fine."

Dawn, however, seemed a lifetime away. Caught in the never-ending cycle of pain, then rest, then pain again, Rose swore that time slowed to the speed of a snail on ice. Her world became her bedroom, the only sounds that of the never-ending rain pelting the roof, her labored breathing and Sullivan's hushed, gentle words of encouragement. He was her rock of strength. In constant contact with her doctor, he sweated through every contraction with her as they gradually increased in intensity, joked with her as she came down from the high of pain, then tenderly wiped the perspiration from her face.

Her defenses down, she stared at him, her eyes roaming over his rugged face, noting the lines of strain that bracketed his mouth when he thought she wasn't watching, the shadows in his green eyes that his lowered lids couldn't quite conceal. He looked tired, as worn out as she felt, but still he tried to tease a smile from her, to take her mind off the fact that her labor wasn't going quite as they had expected. Her contractions were already less than three minutes apart, and dawn wasn't even a promise on the horizon.

He was going to have to deliver her baby.

She let the knowledge curl through her like a breaking wave and braced herself for the fear that was sure to follow in its wake. Instead she realized that while she wanted a doctor with her during the birth of her baby, there was really only one man that she absolutely *needed* there. And that was Sullivan. Because she loved him.

"Rose? Honey?"

Stunned, she glanced up to find him watching her with a frown. Her heart started to thump. Surely he couldn't have read her mind! "What?"

Sullivan gritted his teeth on an oath, wondering how the hell he was going to tell her it didn't look like he was going to be able to keep his promise, after all. She'd probably never trust him again. "I'm sorry," he sighed roughly, tunneling his fingers through his hair for what seemed like the billionth time. "I don't think this baby of yours is going to wait for the helicopter. She seems awfully anxious to put in an appearance."

A smile as soft as morning sunshine flitted across her face and turned her eyes to sapphire. "I know. I'm ready. How about you?"

Just that easily, she gave him her trust. Just that easily, she pulled the rug right out from under him. Would he ever know this woman completely? he wondered, humbled. His throat suddenly thick with emotions, he could only manage a nod before he leaned down to brush a tender kiss across her mouth. When he finally lifted his head, his eyes stung and his smile was crooked. "Dr. Walker told me exactly what to do," he said huskily. "I'm ready when you are."

Twenty minutes later Caitlin Rose MacDonald came into the world kicking and screaming at the top of her lungs, her lusty cries shattering the expectant silence of the bedroom. Unknown tears streaming down his face, Sullivan held the tiny, slippery baby girl in his big hands and grinned broadly. God, she was beautiful!

"You got your wish, love," he rasped, his eyes lifting to Rose's as he gently placed the baby on her stomach. "Say hello to your daughter."

Her eyes filled. "Oh, God," she whispered, blinking back tears. She looked into the baby's tiny, wrinkled face and felt as if she'd been waiting for her all her life. Love, unrestricted and fierce, flowed through her like warm honey. Silently, reverently, with a touch as soft as thistledown, she ran her hands over every inch of her baby, committing her to memory. A laugh escaped her at the feel of her tiny toes, her perfect hands with her perfect nails, the dark, baby-fine hair that was so much like Rose's own. And her heartbeat, she thought in growing wonder as she moved her to the crook of her arm and cradled her against her breast. She could feel her heartbeat thundering beneath her fingers, strong and sure.

Impulsively Rose reached for Sullivan's hand and gently pressed it to the baby's chest. "Feel," she said softly, her eyes glowing as they met his. "Feel how strong and fast it beats. I was so afraid—"

He leaned over and stopped her with a kiss that was quick, sweet, and totally unlike any kiss he had ever given her before. Confused, her heart thundering as fast as the baby's, Rose could only blink, dazed, as he pulled back and said gruffly, "Forget what you were afraid of in the past. Let go of it. The baby's here now and she seems to be perfect, even if she is a little early. Enjoy her."

He would have withdrawn then to give her some time alone with Caitlin, but she held him tight, her blue eyes dark with a love she couldn't have hidden at that moment if her life depended on it. "I haven't thanked you. For everything—for being here for me and the baby. For taking care of both of us. I don't think we would have gotten through it without you—"

"You did all the work," he replied, uncomfortable with her gratitude. "I just gave you a little encouragement."

He'd done a lot more than that, but before Rose could argue the point the rhythmic pounding of helicopter blades seemed to beat the air directly over the house. "There's your ride to the hospital," Sullivan shouted over the noise. "Better late than never. Let's get you and Caitlin cleaned up and ready for company.''

The paramedics rushed in with a stretcher less than ten minutes later and immediately took over. Throwing questions at Sullivan about the birth and any complications that may have arisen, the two men quickly, but efficiently, examined both Rose and the baby, pronounced them in excellent health, and made preparations to transport them to the hospital. With skilled, practiced movements, they wrapped mother and daughter in blankets, carefully shifted Rose to the stretcher, handed her the baby, and strapped them both in. Seconds later they wheeled them out to the waiting helicopter.

It took all of Sullivan's strength of will to let them go. Standing on the back porch, deep lines carving his face, he watched Rose and the baby disappear inside the helicopter. For a fleeting moment he thought he caught a glimpse of Rose's hand lifted in goodbye, but before he could be sure, the door slid shut. The rotating blades whined, picking up speed, and the copter rose into the wet gray sky.

Even before it disappeared from sight, Sullivan felt a sharp, painful tug on his heartstrings. *Go after them.* So strong was the urge, he started toward the porch steps and his pickup before he realized what he was doing. He stopped short, swearing at the empty sky, at the intensity of the emotions that had snuck up on him from out of nowhere. What was the matter with him? He had no right to feel this way about a woman and child who weren't his, a woman and child he tried desperately to convince himself he had no intention of ever making his. If he wasn't damn careful, he was going to get caught up in a wellspring of emotion that a man could happily drown in. And he didn't want that! He'd never wanted that. Somehow he had to find a way to put a stop to the wanting that kept Rose constantly in his mind, the wanting that had somehow become something more than sex, while he still could. Otherwise he was horribly afraid he'd never be able to walk away.

Rose waited expectantly for him to visit her in the hospital that evening. There was so much she had to tell him. The doctor had reported that Caitlin was perfectly formed, and he saw little danger of any complications. But as a precautionary measure, they would keep her in an incubator for a while. The last of her fears evaporating, Rose fed the baby and laughed over her hungry sucking; she'd bathed her and cried at her daintiness, at the clean, wonderful baby scent of her. For what seemed like hours she'd stood at the nursery window and just watched her sleep. And during all those precious moments, the only thing missing had been Sullivan. How many times had she found herself turning to look for him, reaching for the phone to talk to him, wanting to share everything with him? Just in time, she made herself wait. He'll come, she promised herself. Just wait.

But he didn't come that night or the next day when she was released to go home. Pop came instead and took her to a nearby hotel, where she would stay until the baby was allowed to come home the following week. When he'd explained that Sullivan had gotten tied up with a problem at the ranch, she told herself she couldn't expect him to drop everything just to see about her and the baby. She, of all people, knew the demands of running the ranch, and there were times when you just couldn't get away regardless of how badly you wanted to. She would see him tomorrow.

But six tomorrows came and went without any sign of him. Hurt, she couldn't believe that he was actually going to shut her out after the closeness they'd shared during the birth of the baby. There had to be some logical excuse for his behavior, some reason that he couldn't find any time at all to be with her. But then it was time to go home and she could no longer lie to herself. It was Tommy, Slim and Pop who oohed and ahhed over the baby and fussed over her the minute she walked in the door. Only Sullivan kept his distance. Polite as a stranger, he inquired about her health and somehow managed to never quite look at Caitlin even though she was right there in Rose's arms.

Bewildered, her heart throbbing with pain, Rose impatiently waited for supper to be over with her first night home so she could talk to him. But after Pop and the others did the dishes, then reluctantly left, Sullivan gave her no time to demand an explanation. Looking her right in the eye, he announced, "I'll be leaving at dawn on the buying trip we discussed the night before you had the baby. I'll be gone for several weeks."

Eight

He was leaving for the buying trip two weeks early.

Rose almost staggered from the unexpected blow to her heart. This couldn't be happening, she thought wildly, her arms unconsciously tightening around the baby. He couldn't leave her now, not after everything they'd shared. She loved him, for goodness' sake! She always had, though she was only just now coming to realize how much. He'd walked back into her life, back into her heart, as if he'd never left. Surely he knew that. Surely he felt the same way.

But the man who stood before her had the cold, empty eyes of a stranger. This was not the man who cared for her with such gentleness when she was sick. This was not the man who delivered her baby with shaking fingers and held her with his eyes when he laid her daughter in her arms for the first time. This was not a man who would ever want her love, let alone love her.

Suddenly realizing she was losing control, she knew she had to get out of there or she was going to make a complete fool of herself. "I have to put the baby to b-bed," she said shakily. "I'll be right back."

She flew from the room as if the devil himself was after her, her breathing tattered with pain by the time she reached the nursery and gently laid the baby in her cradle. "Get a grip on yourself," she whispered fiercely, blinking back hot, scalding tears. His leaving now could only mean one thing. He was trying to put an immediate stop to the growing intimacy between them.

She wouldn't let him do that to her! To them! Couldn't he see that what they shared was something you could never turn your back on, never leave behind you no matter how far you ran? Somehow she had to find a way to make him see that.

By letting him go.

Her fingers curled around the old, smooth wood of the cradle, instinct urging her to reject the idea without even considering it. As he was so fond of reminding her, she was the boss. She could simply refuse to let him change the original plans. But what would that accomplish in the long run? They didn't have a chance at a future together unless he couldn't stay away.

Later she never knew how she walked back into the kitchen without letting him see that she was taking the biggest chance of her life. She knew she surprised him, she could see it in his eyes. He was obviously waiting for her to demand an explanation, but he waited in vain. All business, she said, "Since we haven't had time to go over the tapes, why don't we do it now? You can also give me an itinerary so I'll know how to reach you just in case something comes up. Not that I'm expecting any problems," she added as she stepped into her office and took the chair behind her desk. "Now that I've had the baby, the boys and I should be able to handle anything unexpected that crops up."

Emotion flickered in his eyes before he could stop it. "The doctor said you shouldn't do anything for the next six weeks."

So he'd been talking to her doctor. Did he realize just how revealing that was? An indifferent man didn't concern himself with the health of a woman he wanted nothing to do with. Fighting to keep the hope out of her voice, she assured him, "I'm not planning to do anything more physical than picking up Caitlin. I just wanted you to know that you don't have to worry about anything here at the ranch while you're gone."

He frowned and jammed a tape into the VCR. "I'm not worried," he growled. "Can we get on with this? I've still got some packing to do."

Biting back a smile that she knew would infuriate him, Rose leaned back in her chair and silently motioned for him to begin.

During the next two weeks Sullivan almost convinced himself he'd done the right thing by leaving as soon as possible after the baby's birth. He had no intention of getting wrapped up in baby smiles and teddy bears the way the rest of the men were. And with a thousand miles or more between him and Rose, he would soon forget the silky smoothness of her skin, the deep blue of her eyes, the smile that could drive a man to drink. He had people to meet, cattle to inspect and buy, transportation to arrange before he moved on to the next big ranch. He wouldn't give Rose a second thought.

That was the way it should have been. But from the day he left her, she'd never been more firmly lodged in his thoughts. A bull grazing in a roadside pasture stirred images of Rose standing in the middle of a country road, nose to nose with Bubba as she tried to lure him to the stock trailer. Hours later he unthinkingly ordered chili at a truck stop outside El Paso and spent the entire meal comparing it to Rose's. It came up irritatingly short. And at his first stop, the Twisted Snake Ranch in New Mexico, wild roses climbed a trellis outside the guest bedroom, the first buds of spring just beginning to bloom. That night Rose came to him in a hot, aching dream that drove everything but the taste and feel of her from his mind. He woke up cursing, and if he could have gotten his hands on her at that moment he would have throttled her.

In the days to come it only got worse as two weeks stretched into three, each longer than the last. The long, lonely stretches of road gave him too much time to think, the long, empty nights too much time to dream of her. Thoughts of her followed him from New Mexico to Colorado to Montana, her constant, invisible presence at his side infuriating him. By the time he conducted the last of his business he was so obsessed with her that he almost started home that very day to demand that she stop tormenting him so. Then he came across a pregnant woman changing a flat all by herself twenty miles outside of Butte. Tall and raw-boned, with long blond hair and hazel eyes, she looked nothing like Rose. But when he stopped to help her, there was something about her uncomplaining willingness to do a man's job when there wasn't one around that reminded Sullivan of dark curly hair and sapphire eyes, of soft, womanly curves that fit so perfectly in his arms. He knew then he couldn't go home. Not without reaching for her the minute he saw her. He was missing her too much. He needed more time.

An hour later he called her from a pay phone at a service station. At the sound of her husky hello his fingers bit into the receiver. "I bought the last of the cattle yesterday," he told her. "They should be arriving in a week or so."

Rose sank down onto a kitchen chair, her legs suddenly unable to hold her. For three long, endless weeks she'd waited for a call that never came, terrified she was losing him. She'd only had to close her eyes to torture herself with images of countless women chasing him, catching him, seducing him. Those were the times she found herself reaching for the phone like a jealous teenager only to slam it back down again. It was his turn to make a move, she'd reminded herself. As time dragged on, she'd nearly given up hope that he would.

Her heart dancing to a wild beat, she struggled to adopt his businesslike tone as she asked, "Then you're on your way home?"

He hesitated, then finally admitted, "No."

Pain, unlike anything she had ever known, squeezed her chest until she could hardly breathe. So this was it. He was calling to tell her he wasn't coming back. Oh, God, why hadn't anyone warned her that the hurt was always worse the second time? Her voice thick with hurt, she whispered, ''Why not?''

Because you're all I can think about. Because you scare the hell out of me. Because you're getting to me again and I can't let that happen, he wanted to shout. Instead he gave her the excuse he'd worked out before he called her. It was a legitimate one, but still an excuse nevertheless. ''We're going to need more men once roundup starts. I didn't figure you'd want to hire the hands who walked out on you when you fired Hastings, so I thought I'd scout around up here and see who might be available. Montana roundups are later than ours, and I know quite a few good men who could use the work while they're waiting for their spring. That is, of course, if it's all right with you,'' he added stiffly. ''It's your ranch.''

Rose, reeling with disappointment and loneliness, hardly heard the curious desperation in the words he had once thrown at her like an accusation, as if he were trying with all his might to hang onto his resentment. ''Of course it's all right,'' she replied. ''You're the foreman. Hire whoever you want. I trust you.''

He froze, guilt, unexpected and swift, nearly choking him. *Don't!* He wanted to caution her. *Five weeks ago the only thought in my head was doing whatever it took to get back what was mine. The last thing you should give me is your trust.*

"Sullivan? Did you hear me? When will you be home?"

He blinked, snapping back to attention. "I don't know—a couple of weeks, maybe. However long it takes me to round up some men."

A couple of weeks. Rose almost groaned. He might as well have said an eternity, but she couldn't complain. At least he was still planning to return.

In the weeks to come, loneliness took on a whole new meaning for Rose. When the baby was awake, all her energy was devoted to loving her, caring for her, building that special bond between a mother and child that lasts a lifetime. But Caitlin was a wonderful baby; she slept for hours at a time. During those quiet, endless moments Rose found herself starving for just the sight of Sullivan. Drawn like a magnet to the window that looked out on the foreman's house at the bottom of the hill, she stared at the empty, abandoned house and missed him in a way that terrified her. When had she come to need his presence in her life so much?

Then, suddenly, without warning, he was home. Arriving early one evening with the ten cowboys he'd brought with him, he strode into the kitchen just as Rose and the hands were sitting down for supper. Pandemonium broke out. Pop, Slim and Tommy greeted him as if he was a long lost brother, introductions were made, and amid all the laughter and catching up on news, more places were set at the table.

In the crowd of men, no one noticed that Rose didn't join in the conversation much as she whisked one of the casseroles she kept in the freezer for just such unexpected arrivals into the microwave. She shook hands with each of the newcomers and welcomed them to her home, but she had eyes for only one man. Hungrily, her gaze roamed over him, devouring him. Was he leaner? Harder? Dressed in snugfitting jeans and a white cotton shirt open at the collar, there wasn't an ounce of fat on him anywhere. He laughed at something Pop said, the crooked smile that turned up one corner of his mouth unconsciously wicked, unbearably tempting. Tracing it with her eyes, Rose felt her heartbeat quicken, her blood thicken and heat. Six weeks, she thought, dazed. It had been six weeks since he had kissed her. It seemed like a lifetime.

He looked up abruptly, finding her unerringly in the roomful of tall men. Her heart lurched to a stop, the heat in his green eyes almost melting her knees. He didn't say a word, made no move to come to her, but she felt as if he touched her, stroked her, wrapped her close in his arms. Need. The urgency was there in his eyes, stark and bare, a silent testament of long days and even longer nights, of loneliness and desolation and too much time to think.

She wanted to run to him then, to throw herself into his arms and never let him go. But she couldn't. She wasn't the young, vulnerable girl she had been at eighteen, so insecure and starving for love that she'd misjudged first his, then Frank's feelings for her. She had given him her heart, only to have it trampled under his feet as he left town. She wouldn't make that mistake again. She loved him more than she'd ever thought possible, but if all he wanted from her was revenge, then she wouldn't let him use that love as a weapon to destroy her. Not this time.

At his side, Pop gave him a running account of everything he'd missed while he was gone, but Sullivan couldn't tear his gaze from Rose. She'd lost weight. He'd noticed it the minute he stepped through the back door and almost tripped over his own feet in surprise. She was as slim as a girl, her slender hips provokingly encased in jeans, her narrow waist hardly bigger than the span of his hands. With slow deliberateness he took his gaze higher to the full curve of her breasts concealed beneath her blue checked blouse. Did she know how he ached to feel the weight of her breasts in his palms? How he burned with the remembered feel of her hips melting into his? If he could just touch her...

He'd lose his head completely, he thought resentfully. After six weeks of torturous dreams, it would take nothing more than the brush of his skin against hers to destroy what little control he still had left where she was concerned. Infuriated by the very idea of it, he somehow found the strength to turn away.

Rose didn't doubt for a minute that he'd done it deliberately. After the way he had managed to put her out of his life for the last six weeks, she should have been prepared for it. They were back to being polite strangers.

She wasn't going to let him get away with it, she decided. Not after all they had shared. He could lie to himself all he wanted, but if he thought she was going to make it easy for him by going along with him, he was nuts. She loved him and it was high time she found out how he really felt about her.

But for the next two days he neatly sidestepped all her attempts to talk to him alone. Then roundup started, and suddenly there weren't enough hours in the day for everything that needed to get done.

When Frank had added the Lazy J to his own holdings, he'd used Jeeps and helicopters to gather the cows and new calves, reducing the operation to one of money-saving, practical efficiency. Sullivan, however, came from a long line of cowboys and wranglers who had clung to the ways of the past and the skills they had perfected only after long hours of practice in the saddle. There would be no Jeeps or helicopters at any roundup he was in charge of, no modern technology to ruin what was considered by most old hands as the highlight of the year.

Consequently the warm spring days were filled with hot, dusty work from sunup to sundown. There were horses to be broken, cows and calves to be rounded up then separated, branding and inoculations to be done. The old chuck wagon stored in the barn at the Lazy J was hauled out, cleaned up, and loaded down with enough supplies to feed an army. Pop hitched it up to an ornery mule named Trouble and followed the men around the huge ranch, taking over the duties of cook for Rose, since she could hardly cook on an open camp fire when she had a baby to tend to. Then at night the cowboys slept under the stars, just like in the old days, grumbling about rocks that didn't show themselves until after midnight and ground as hard as granite. But not one of them would have traded his sleeping bag for a bed in the bunkhouse.

Rose only saw the men when she was able to join them for meals. Even then, Sullivan kept his distance. She tried to tell herself it was probably for the best, but the hurt was still there—a constant pain in the region of her heart that only seemed to intensify rather than diminish with the passing of time. Still she didn't avoid the nightly gathering around the camp fire. She couldn't, so she simply ceased to try. Bundling up the baby against the cool night air, she usually arrived in time for supper, then stayed for just a little while to listen to the inevitable stories and tall tales that circled the fire as the men began to unwind.

The third night of the roundup, however, the laughter and easy conversation that followed the meal was slightly strained. Everything that could have gone wrong that day had, and the men were tired and sore. From across the camp Rose watched Sullivan through the dancing flames of the camp fire. His face shadowed, his thoughts well hidden behind his shuttered green eyes, he looked like a man who had stepped out of time, a man who knew little of civilization. His hair as dark as midnight, his jaw stubbled with whiskers, he could have been a rogue, a scoundrel, an outlaw lover.

Fascinated, entranced, Rose pictured herself going to him, easing the grim set of his sensuous mouth, kneading the tension from his stiff shoulders, touching the heat she knew lingered just under warm skin that had been bronzed by the firelight. When she grew hot just thinking about it, she knew it was time to leave.

Her heart pounding, she pushed to her feet and lifted the baby from the Portacrib Pop kept for her in the chuck wagon. Hugging Caitlin to her breast, she said, "I guess we'll call it a night. You guys look like you've had a rough day and need your sleep. We'll see you tomorrow."

There were a few halfhearted protests, and what had become routine good-night kisses for Caitlin, who had been adopted by just about every one of the men. But before Rose could move to her truck, Tommy called out, "Hey, Sullivan, you should go back to the house with Rose and let her look at your shoulder. That was a pretty nasty fall you took."

"Fall?" she echoed, her eyes wide in her suddenly pale face as she pivoted to search out Sullivan in the darkness. "What happened?"

He shot Tommy a look that could have coated the boy's vocal chords with ice. "Nothing. It was just a little accident."

Tommy snorted at that, blindly ignoring Sullivan's efforts to shut him up. "He was breaking that mean-looking sorrel and got thrown into the fence. It ripped his shirt right off his back."

Her gaze swiveled back to Sullivan's. "Were you cut?" she asked in alarm. "Maybe you should come up to the house and let me take a look at it. You may need a tetanus shot."

"It's just a scratch," he argued. "And I don't need another tetanus shot. I just had one six months ago."

"You still shouldn't take any chances on it getting infected." Her jaw set as stubbornly as his, she headed for the truck. "It needs to be cleaned and bandaged. Come on."

Caught in the gaze of thirteen interested pairs of eyes, Sullivan knew if he didn't go with her, someone was going to start wondering why he suddenly didn't want to be alone with her. Muttering a curse under his breath, he had no choice but to trail after her, promising himself with every step that he was going to keep this short and sweet.

But once they reached the house, she had to change Caitlin and put her to bed. Standing in he kitchen, Sullivan heard her soft murmurings to the baby, then the husky cadence of a whispered lullaby. He felt something deep inside him soften and give, the hard edge that always gave him the advantage blurring. He took a step toward the nursery, then another one, unable to resist the lure of her voice.

The minute he stepped into the open doorway, he knew he'd made a mistake. She stood at the window, her dark head bent to the baby's as she slowly swayed to the tune she hummed, the soft glow of the night-light wrapping both her and the baby in grainy, dreamlike shadows. Transfixed, drawn to her in spite of the alarm bells suddenly ringing wildly in his head, he couldn't turn away from an image he would carry with him to his grave.

Unaware of his presence, Rose gently laid the baby in her cradle and brushed a kiss across her petal-soft cheek. Whispering a soft good-night, she turned toward the door and stopped short at the sight of Sullivan watching her, his narrowed, intense gaze holding hers in the dark. Suddenly the night air was humming.

Silently she started toward him, easing past him as he stepped back only a fraction to grant her passage through the doorway. But instead of showing him to the back door as her common sense screamed for her to do, she wordlessly moved to the bathroom. The firm tread of his booted feet on the carpet assured her he was right behind her.

Her pulse quickened, scattering heat through her veins. But she was all business as she switched on the light and flipped down the toilet seat. "Take off your shirt and sit down." Not sparing him a glance, she pivoted toward the medicine cabinet for the antibiotic cream she kept there for minor scratches.

Tending his cuts should have been that simple. But when she turned back from the medicine cabinet, the tube of cream in her hand, she found herself confronting the naked expanse of his broad back. Her heart jerked to a surprised halt, then stumbled into a desperate, frantic beat that she was sure he could hear in the sudden, expectant silence. Say something, she told herself. Anything!

"Well? How is it?" he demanded in a gravelly voice when she made no move to touch the scratches the barbed wire had carved in his back.

How was it? Her throat as dry as a West Texas creekbed in the middle of summer, she couldn't have answered if her life had depended on it. How was she supposed to describe a strength, a power, that made her go weak at the knees? Her fingers, itching to explore, to caress, lifted to the angry red welts that marred his right shoulder.

The stroke of her fingers, as light and airy as a feather, sizzled through Sullivan like an unexpected charge of electricity. His spine snapped ramrod straight, his teeth clamping down on a moan of sheer frustration.

Alarmed, Rose snatched her hand back. "I'm sorry! I didn't mean to hurt you."

An ironic laugh nearly choked him. Didn't she know by now that just the sight of her made him hurt? "Just get on with it," he growled. "I'll live."

But would she? Being this close to him, having free rein to run her hands over his back, even if it was under the guise of cleaning his wounds, was almost more than she could bear. With infinite care she washed each scratch, each scrape, and applied the soothing cream, her hair brushing his shoulder, her breath warming his skin as she leaned close. Once she thought she heard him swear, but she couldn't be sure because he never took his eyes from the white ceramic toothbrush holder he broodingly stared at.

Then, all too soon, she was finished. She should have stepped back, should have wished him goodnight and escaped to her room. Instead, as if of their own volition, her fingers lifted to the nape of his neck and slowly traced the dark edge of his hair.

Heat arrowed from her fingers straight to his loins. He froze, but only for an instant. Before she could guess his intentions, he swiveled around sharply and caught her in the act of moving closer, her fingers lifted to repeat the caress. Suddenly she was standing between his open thighs and neither could have said how she got there. "What the hell do you think you're doing?"

Answering without saying a word, a single finger skimmed over his shoulder with defiant tenderness, lingered at the curve of his collarbone, then trailed liquid fire to the pulse that hammered at the base of his throat.

His eyes closed on a groan. "I'm warning you, Rose. I'm in no mood to play games."

But this wasn't a game. She was deadly serious. She still didn't have any idea where she stood with him. He could use her, then walk away for good. But she couldn't think about the future when he was this close, couldn't worry about what revenge he might have planned when the only thing that mattered was the taste of his mouth on hers, the feel of his hard body pressed tightly against hers.

"Feel my heartbeat," she whispered, swaying toward him. "Then try to tell me I'm playing."

No! Later he never knew if he was trying to deny her or himself, but it ceased to matter the minute he clamped his hands on her hips, jerking her to him as he turned his head against her breast. Still standing, she arched against him with an inarticulate cry of surprise, her heart thundering wildly beneath his mouth.

"Tell me to stop," he groaned, his hot breath and the flick of his tongue sweetly puckering her nipple beneath the white cotton of her shirt. But she only melted into him with a whimper, her fingers tunneling into his hair to hold him closer. A shudder ran through him, hunger, hot and insatiable, making a mockery of his last-ditch efforts to hang onto reason. His hands, ignoring the dictates of his mind, were already moving, already relearning the intoxicating flare of her hips and reclaiming a waist that had no business being that small only six weeks after having a baby.

Impatiently, like a man starving for the feel of her, he tugged her shirt free of her jeans and spread his fingers over the smooth, flawless skin of her back. *Soft.* Damn, why did she have to be so soft? A man could sink right into her and lose himself before he ever thought to note the danger. He had to stop. Why wasn't she helping him stop?

Desperate, desire clawing at him, he pushed her back abruptly and surged to his feet. But even then he couldn't bring himself to let her go. Holding her in front of him, her breasts nearly brushing his chest, he struggled to think of a reason—any reason—why he shouldn't carry her into her bedroom and make love to her the way he was burning to. "The baby," he ground out, drawing her up on her toes until her mouth was just a promise away from his. "It's too soon after the baby. I don't want to hurt you."

She clutched at him, the only thought in her passion-clouded mind that of pleasing him. Hadn't Frank taught her that a man never drew back, never had any problems in bed, as long as his woman pleased him? She pressed her mouth to his, a quick, fleeting kiss that teased and tantalized for a second, two at the most, before she drew back scant inches, changed the angle and teased him all over again. "I'm fine," she huskily breathed into his mouth. "The doctor's already cleared me to resume all activities. Let me show you...."

She gave him no time to think, to argue, to even begin to withdraw. She forgot where they were, who they were, only that she couldn't let him stop. Not tonight. Every touch, every kiss, every teasing dart of her tongue was designed to drive him mad with pleasure, to pull his unresisting body into the hot, swirling eddies of desire. Murmuring his name over and over, she scattered kisses across his face and throat as her fingers blindly searched out the buttons to his shirt, then moved on to the snap of his jeans.

Something was wrong. Through the passion that dulled his brain, the thought nagged at him. She moved over him like a cat lapping up cream, but somehow he sensed it was *his* desires that drove her, *his* need that she sought to satisfy. She took nothing for herself.

Drowning in the taste of her, he wrenched his mouth from hers, his breathing ragged as he frowned down at her. "Honey—"

She rubbed her hips against his, her hands almost desperate as they slipped around his neck and tried to pull him back down to her. "Tell me what you want," she pleaded anxiously. "I can make it good for you. Just tell me—"

He silenced her by simply pressing his fingers to her lips, the suspicions that stirred in him unwanted, unacceptable. His frown darkened to a black scowl. "Sweetheart, why would you think it's your responsibility to make it good for me? I thought we were in this together."

She blinked, surprised that he even had to ask. "We are, but what kind of woman would I be if I couldn't please you?"

"What kind of wo—" he sputtered to a stop, suddenly wanting to kill a man who was already beyond his reach. Drawing back carefully, he said, "Tell me about Frank, honey. About your life with him."

"Now?"

"Right now. I've got a feeling this is something we should have discussed a long time ago."

She didn't want to tell him. Not now. Not ever. But she knew that look in Sullivan's eye. He wasn't budging until she told him what he wanted to know. Swallowing the pain that was already rising in her throat, she began.

She told him everything, leaving nothing out. Her voice wobbly with pain, she told him of her despair when her father died, the terrible loneliness and fear that had gripped her when it suddenly hit her that she was totally and completely alone in the world. If Frank hadn't been there, she would have been lost. She had thought she'd loved him then—he was always there for her, protecting her, promising he would always be there. When he had pressed for marriage, she'd thought they could find happiness together. But she hadn't known then why he'd wanted to marry her.

Sullivan's hands tightened on her arms as he listened to her tell him how Frank had used her to get back at him; how she'd tried to make her marriage work and blamed herself when it was never quite right; how Frank had not only let her carry the guilt for their less than satisfactory sex life, he'd encouraged her every step of the way.

A rage unlike anything he had ever known before filled him. Spitting out a curse, he leaned down and swept her up in his arms as if she were as fragile as spun glass. "Forget what Frank told you, sweetheart. The man never did know his ass from a hole in the ground. Making love isn't about one person making it good for the other. It's about sharing and giving and receiving. We make it good for each other. You got that?"

Her mouth so close he could feel the startled puff of her moist breath, she nodded. "Good," he said in satisfaction, heading for her bedroom. "Then let's go to bed."

Nine

He laid her on the bed with the utmost care, promising himself he would make this a night she would never forget. But the minute he came down to her, the minute his mouth covered hers and she wrapped her arms around him as if she would never let him go, the only thought in his head was Rose. Rose, with her petal-smooth skin that heated like honey under his hands. Rose, her legs moving restlessly, sensuously beneath his, her breath shattering on a moan of sheer frustration as she fought buttons and zippers and jeans that were suddenly too confining. Rose, somehow as naked as he, dissolving at the touch of his hand at her breast, her hip, the tender, sensitive skin of her inner thigh. Rose, who seemed so surprised that this first time, after all their years apart, was for her.

Drowning in a pleasure that was dark and intoxicating, she tried to stop him long enough to catch her breath, tried to remind him that he'd just told her that they were supposed to make it good for each other. But he wouldn't listen. The very second she opened her mouth, he gave her a slow, lazy, languid kiss, and rational thought skittered away.

Need. She had thought she'd known the boundaries of it even with him. But the last time she'd made love with him, she had been little more than a girl, with a girl's dreams, a girl's needs. And what she'd shared with Frank had been nothing like this. This blurred the edges of reason, caressed the soul, pushed her toward a heat that seared, consumed, released. Her breath catching on a sob, she clung to him, his name on her lips a desperate, whispered call in the night.

"Easy, honey," he murmured against her throat. "We've got all night."

But she was hot now. Aching now. Dying for more now. She reached for him, her fingers sliding down the lean, muscled plane of his chest, past his trim waist to the hard, burning proof of his desire. "Please! I need..."

In a heartbeat she was flat on her back and he was between her thighs, pressing her into the sheets. In the darkness his green eyes met hers, his lungs gasping for the air she had stolen from him with her hand. He could take her now. With a deep thrust he could end the agony tearing at him and sheath himself in her sweet heat. But it was much too soon. He wanted her boneless, mindless with desire, the fire he knew raged in her belly burning her with a pleasure that destroyed all memories of any other man who had ever touched her.

Slowly, deliberately, he attacked her senses, playfully teasing her one moment, then dragging her down deeper into passion the next. Reality shifted and changed until it consisted of nothing more than the feel of his hands working their magic on her, the thunder of his heart beating in time with hers, his low, growling whisper as he murmured erotic words of praise in her ear. Tension gathered in her stomach, coiling tighter and tighter until she thought she would shatter into a million pieces if he didn't come to her soon.

''Sullivan!''

Her agonized cry destroyed him. There was no more time for teasing, no more time for drawing out a pleasure that had suddenly come too close to pain. Lifting her hips, he eased into her with maddening slowness, the groan that vibrated through him coming from his very soul. Just that easily, he rediscovered a completeness he'd never found with any other woman.

That would worry the hell out of him when he had time to think about it. But for now his body begged for release, demanded it. Tenderly, savagely, he stroked her again and again, stoking the wet heat inside her until it flamed out of control so quickly she gasped in surprise. Her nails raked his back. At the very core of her, he felt her splinter, the ecstasy that rippled through her like lightning destroying the last fine threads of his control. Impossibly his already thundering heart quickened, his muscles tightened, his hips surged powerfully against hers. Before he could catch his breath, pleasure exploded in him as wave after wave of ecstasy rolled over him.

"I love you."

A long while later the words were hardly more than a whisper in the darkness, a shy murmur half concealed in the shadows. But Sullivan stiffened as if she'd screamed them, as if she was making a demand of him he couldn't meet. Guilt pounded him, sickened him. This was what he thought he'd wanted, he told himself furiously, the revenge he'd planned from the beginning. Where was the elation? The triumph? He should have been doing handsprings, making plans to rush her into marriage so he could get his ranch back. Instead all he could think of was how much she'd hate him if she ever found out the truth.

His hand sliding over her back in a caress he couldn't deny himself, he warned roughly, "Don't love me, honey. You'll only get hurt because I can't love you back."

She stilled, her heart seeming to stop. *Don't,* she wanted to cry. *Don't do this to me, to us, a second time. I know you love me. I felt it pouring out of you only moments ago.* But the words wouldn't come. Instead she asked the one question she swore she wouldn't. "Why?"

"Because loving a woman like you means marriage, kids, the whole nine yards," he replied quietly. Bitterness crept into his voice along with something she hadn't heard before—acceptance. It terrified her.

"I have nothing to offer you. Nothing except lust, and that's not enough."

"That's not true!" She clutched at him, wanting to shake him, wanting to cling to him. He hadn't moved, hadn't made any move to withdraw, but the panic rising in her told her she was losing him. "Why are you doing this?" she demanded. "Why are you trying to pretend you don't love me? I know you do—"

"Know this," he growled, his green eyes snaring hers in the darkness as he deliberately moved against her, letting her feel the extent of his arousal. "I want you more than I ever wanted anyone. Feel that? No one has ever made me want this bad, this hard, this long. It's all I have to give you. Let it be enough."

"But—"

He didn't want to argue. Not now, not when this was all he would ever have of her. Taking her mouth in a hot, carnal kiss, he swept her back into the hot, blinding flames of passion before she could summon another word of protest.

The next morning he was gone when she awoke, the tender ache between her thighs the only sign that the night had been more than a dream. Disappointed that he wasn't there to share the dawn with her, she pictured the night to come, when they could be together again, and smiled dreamily up at the ceiling. This time, she promised herself, there would be no talk of lust, no running from the truth. She would find a way to make him admit that what he felt for her was too strong, too binding, too complete, to be anything but love.

But when she saw him at lunch, he acted as if the night had never happened, as if they hadn't shared a passion that had nearly set the sheets on fire, as if she was nothing more to him than the woman who signed his paycheck. Stricken, she felt the pain hit her first, the force of it nearly staggering her. Then came the anger. Sharp and bracing, it brought her chin up and burned like a fire in the depths of her eyes. Did he think she didn't know what he was doing? He was cutting her out of his heart, denying them both any chance of happiness because of his stubborn pride.

Five years ago she'd accepted his abandonment of her because she'd thought she had no other choice. She had accepted whatever fate and the men in her life had decided to give her because she'd thought there could be nothing worse than being alone. Now she knew better. Now she knew that you could be married to the wrong man and still be alone. Now she knew that second chances were rare, a precious gift not to be squandered away because of self-doubts or fears. If she wanted Sullivan, she would have to fight for him. Because if she didn't, if she let him get away with ignoring her now, she knew he would never touch her again.

It didn't take Sullivan long to realize that war had been declared and *he* was under siege. During the next two weeks, as roundup ended and life returned to normal, Rose took advantage of every opportunity to touch him. With an innocent smile that did nothing to conceal the challenge sparkling in her blue eyes, she brushed up against him when he least expected it, her body softly tantalizing his for only an instant before she was gone, leaving him with nothing more than the seductive scent of her perfume and the pounding of his heart to assure him he hadn't dreamed the whole thing.

Irritated at the response he couldn't quite control, he found himself watching for her, waiting for her, bracing himself for her subtle torture. But she was clever, he had to give her that. Her attacks were always well-timed and geared for surprise, and she didn't give a hoot in hell who was watching. She walked up behind him when he was talking to Pop and scraped her nail teasingly along the sensitive skin above his collar, drawing a scowl from him and a speculative grin from the older man. One hot afternoon she and Caitlin showed up at the windmill he was helping Tommy and Slim repair and announced she was going into town for supplies. Bold as brass, she drew her fingers all the way down the buttons of his shirt to the snap of his jeans and asked him if he needed anything. Slim and Tommy nearly dropped their teeth, and he was reaching for her before he realized she'd slipped away with a soft laugh.

No, the woman didn't play fair. She knew she was wearing down his resistance, but did she show him any mercy? Hell, no! He was frustrated, his indifference in shambles, but she didn't give an inch. Then she brought in the big gun. Caitlin. How did she know he couldn't ignore that baby even though he tried his damnedest? He never touched her, never played with her like the other hands did, never allowed himself to hold her close as he longed to. But she didn't make a

move in her crib that he didn't know about whenever
he was in the house.

But that wasn't enough for Rose. She saw the longing in his eyes when he watched the baby from a safe
distance, the love he wouldn't admit to, let alone allow himself to give. Taking matters into her own
hands, she decided to do something about it one evening after supper when he stayed to catch up on paperwork.

Up to her elbows in the mountain of dirty baby
clothes that piled up after just one day, she was trans-
ferring just-washed diapers from the washer to the
dryer when she heard Caitlin start to fuss in her play-
pen. As usual her first reaction was to drop everything and run to her, but this time she forced herself
to stay where she was. Sullivan was in her office and
much closer to the baby than she was. "Sullivan, will
you see about the baby for me?" she called out. "I've
got my hands full."

For a moment her only answer was dead silence and
the steadily increasing whispers of the baby. Disappointed, she was halfway across the laundry room
when he asked in a voice raised in growing panic,
"What do I do? How do I make her stop crying?"

Rose grinned. "Pick her up, but make sure you
support her head. If she acts hungry, she has a bottle
in the refrigerator."

Pick her up! Sullivan stared down at the red-faced
baby in horror. He'd held her at birth, but that had
been different. He hadn't had time to think about
supporting her head or how small she was; he'd just
acted on instinct. His heart beating jerkily in his chest,

he leaned over and gingerly placed one hand beneath her small bottom and the other at the back of her curly head.

The minute he painstakingly lifted her to his chest, her crying ceased. Her deep blue eyes alight with what he would have sworn was recognition, she stared up at him silently, her tiny mouth forming an *O* of surprise. Emotion flooded Sullivan, a sweetness unlike anything he had known before, and in that instant he knew he was lost. He didn't give a damn who her father had been, whose name she carried. He delivered her and that made her part his.

"Well, hello, sweetheart," he sighed as he carefully transferred her to the crook of his arm and smiled down at her. God, she was tiny! "Your mama says you're hungry. What do you say?"

For an answer, she put her fist in her mouth.

A crooked smile tugged up one corner of his mouth. "Looks like she was right. Let's go get you a bottle."

From the laundry room Rose heard his soft whispers, the sound of his booted feet crossing the kitchen to the refrigerator, then returning to the nursery. After that there was only silence. Listening to the hushed quiet, Rose started the dryer and began to sort another load of clothes for the washer. By the time she'd added soap and fabric softener, her curiosity was killing her. On silent feet she slipped to the open door of the nursery.

Not sure what to expect, she stopped short at the sight of Sullivan holding Caitlin close, her sleeping face turned against his chest as he sat in the straight-back kitchen chair that was a poor substitute for the rocker she had yet to find. Blinking back sudden tears, her heart filled with love as her eyes met his. "She's asleep," she whispered. "You can lay her down now."

His voice as low as hers, he looked down helplessly at the baby and said, "I was afraid I'd wake her up."

Rose couldn't help but smile, understanding perfectly. There were times when just holding her was so sweet she couldn't put her down, even when she knew she would sleep more comfortably in her own bed. "Nothing short of an atomic bomb will wake her up once she's really asleep," she assured him quietly. "Go ahead. Just lay her on her tummy and pat her back and she'll never know a thing."

His heart pounding, he did as she said, half expecting Caitlin to let out a jarring yell of protest any moment. But she didn't blink a single tiny eyelash when he tenderly lowered her to the crib. With a touch so light it was little more than a whisper of movement, he gently patted her back.

Rose never knew how long they stood there side by side, watching the baby sleep. In the hushed stillness she could almost feel love pouring from Sullivan in an unconscious flow, warming both her and Caitlin, claiming them. She also felt the exact moment he realized it. He stiffened suddenly and stepped back jerkily, away from her, away from the baby, away from the emotions he was still so determined to deny.

"I have to go," he said tightly. "It's late." And before she could even open her mouth to tell him goodnight, he was gone.

She didn't go after him. Not then or the next day, when she didn't see hide nor hair of him. He was running scared, and she had to believe that a man only ran that scared when he was fighting a losing battle. Hopefully, given enough time and space, he would see that.

Her patience, however, gave out by the middle of the second day. He filled her thoughts and destroyed her concentration by simply avoiding her for hours. And she wasn't going to let him get away with it. Leaving the baby with Tommy's sister, Maryann, who baby-sat for her one day a week while she ran errands, she went looking for him.

He was supposed to be at the Lazy J putting in a late alfalfa crop for feed for next winter. But the field he'd spent the last week preparing and plowing was deserted, the tractor abandoned midway down a long furrow. She frowned, wondering if she was going to have to search every inch of the old ranch to find him when she suddenly caught a glimpse of his pickup parked in the shade of the huge, towering cypress trees bordering the river at the far end of the pasture. Shifting her own truck into gear, she headed straight for it.

She expected to find him sitting on the bank by the slow-moving river, eating the sandwiches he now packed each morning for lunch so he could avoid coming back to the house—and her—every day at noon. But he wasn't by the river; he was *in* it.

Braking to an abrupt stop next to his truck, Rose cut the engine and stepped down to the grassy ground, her eyes lingering on the clothes and boots carelessly discarded on the bank. From there, she only had to look to the river to find Sullivan. He stood up to his bronzed chest in the dark green water, his black hair plastered to his head and water sluicing down his shoulders and arms as if he had just surfaced. He looked magnificent. He also looked irritated as hell that she had chanced upon him with his pants down.

Making no attempt to hide the slow grin that pulled at her mouth, she strolled toward him, wicked amusement spilling into her eyes. "Hi. How's the water?"

His eyes, as green as the river, narrowed. "Cool," he retorted curtly. "What are you doing here?"

"Looking for you. We need to talk."

The last thing they needed to do when he was naked as the day he was born was talk! "Save it for later. I'm busy."

"So I can see," she chuckled. Gracefully she sank down to the bank and slipped her arms around her updrawn knees, as if she intended to stay awhile. "I'm serious, Sullivan. This is important."

Sullivan swore in frustration. The woman gave new meaning to the word stubborn. "If it's that important, go on back to the house and I'll meet you there in a few—"

"I want you to be Caitlin's godfather."

The simple request, hardly spoken above a whisper, took the wind right out of his sails. Rocked to the soles of his feet, he stared at her blankly. "What?"

She smiled, encouraged that he hadn't immediately given an out-and-out no. "I want you to be Caitlin's godfather," she repeated, looking him straight in the eye. "You brought her into the world. You were there when she drew her first breath. Maryann, Tommy's sister, is going to be her godmother but Caitlin needs a man in her life, someone she can depend on to be there for her if something happens to me. I want that man to be you."

Emotion—surprise, joy, fear, fury—whipped through him. She was asking too much, he tried to tell himself, grasping at weak straws of anger. He wouldn't let her play on the possessiveness that had gripped him from the moment the baby had slipped into his hands at birth. He wouldn't let her tie the three of them into a neat little family package when that was the last thing they could ever be.

"Nothing's going to happen to you," he replied stiffly.

"Probably not," she agreed. "But it's important to me that you'll always be a part of Caitlin's life. You don't have to decide now, but will you at least think about it?"

He hesitated, knowing he was making a mistake, but the words of refusal wouldn't come. "All right," he said grudgingly. "I'll think about it. But that's it. I'm not making any promises."

She flashed him a smile that was as bright as the sunlight that filtered through the leaves overhead and jumped to her feet. "Good. Now that that's settled—" Making a sudden decision, her fingers moved to the buttons of her yellow camp blouse.

Sullivan's heart shot up into his throat. "What the hell do you think you're doing?"

"Going swimming," she said innocently. "I'm hot."

Hot? He'd give her hot, he thought furiously. Hot was when you were standing up to your armpits in cold water and steam was starting to rise from certain body parts! "The hell you are," he grated. "Dammit, Rose, put that blouse back on! One of the men could come by and see you."

Grinning, she held the offending garment between her thumb and index finger and casually dropped it on top of his clothes. "The men have all gone to town," she retorted. "I gave them the rest of the afternoon off." Her blue eyes locked with his, she reached for the snap of her jeans and pushed it free. In the next instant the slow rasp of her zipper teased the sudden, tense silence.

Sullivan's jaw hardened as he refused to let his gaze drop to the path of her descending zipper. "I'm warning you," he snarled. "If you don't stop this instant—"

"You'll what?" she tossed back, softly goading him. "Come out of the water and stop me yourself?"

"Yes, dammit!"

Her zipper, grating loudly, called his bluff.

He was out of the water like a shot, moving so fast Rose didn't even have a chance to catch her breath before he was upon her, reaching for her, yanking her flush against his wet, aroused body the same instant his lips covered hers. She gasped, and that was the only advantage he needed. His tongue surged into the dark, moist recesses of her mouth, stealing her breath, her will, seducing her, telling her without words all the mad, passionate things he intended to do to her.

His hands rushed over her, wild and reckless, trembling with need. He fumbled with the clasp of her bra, only to swear against her mouth when he couldn't manage to release the hooks. "Help me!" he pleaded, wrenching his mouth from hers.

She moaned, his urgency catching her and sending the earth spinning away beneath her feet. Her fingers nudged his. A gasp, a sob, a muffled curse later, the clasp was nearly ripped from its binding and the bra went flying. Rose never saw, never cared, where it landed. Fiercely returning his kiss, she rubbed against him, loving the feel of him, the heat of him, the subtle friction of wet skin against dry. She heard his groan, felt his fingers flex at her waist as he dragged her closer still, and then he was reaching for her jeans.

He was going too fast. The thought registered dully somewhere in a dark corner of his brain, but he couldn't stop, couldn't even begin to curb the fever blazing out of control in his blood. Tearing his mouth from hers, he tugged down the zipper she had teased him with, his labored breath tearing through lungs that suddenly couldn't get enough air. With a rough jerk, he dragged her jeans over her hips and down her thighs. Before she'd kicked them free, he was reaching for her again, sweeping her panties from her, and lowering her to the sweet-smelling grass of the riverbank.

High overhead, the tops of the cypress trees swayed gently to a slight breeze, but flat on her back, Rose had eyes for no one but Sullivan. She loved him! She wanted to tell him, intended to keep telling him until he opened his heart to her and admitted that he loved her, too. But not now. Now she couldn't manage more than a groan of need when he ironed kisses along her jaw and down her throat to her breast. Latching onto her nipple with his mouth, his hand joined the attack on her senses, sliding up her thigh to the heart of her desire. He touched her and she whimpered, her thoughts clouding, her mind closing out everything but each gliding stroke of his fingers, each gentle, tender tug of his mouth.

A sob of pleasure escaping her parted lips, she arched up like a tightly strung bow, offering herself to him, opening to him. "Now," she panted brokenly, crying out. "Please—"

At that moment, caught in the loving heat of her gaze, Sullivan knew he never would be able to deny her anything she asked of him. Groaning her name thickly, he took her wildly, hotly, completely. And somewhere in the taking, in the satisfying of a desire that no woman but this one had ever been able to quench in him, he gave his heart and never felt the loss until it was too late.

Ten

Dawn broke on the horizon and washed the cloudless sky in muted shades of lavender and pink. Standing at his bedroom window, Sullivan never noticed the beginning of what promised to be a perfect spring day. Instead his eyes were trained on the house on the hill, his face set in grim lines. How had he let things get so far out of hand? he wondered in bewilderment. He was quickly sinking into what could only turn out to be a disaster, and everything he did to extricate himself only pulled him deeper and deeper into the quagmire.

How had she tricked him into agreeing to being Caitlin's godfather? He'd never actually said yes. But then again, he'd never actually said no, either, he reluctantly admitted. He'd been waiting for her to exert some sort of pressure on him, but in the week that had passed since they'd made love by the river, she had done nothing of the kind. She'd just assumed that he would accept. How had she known that his heart wouldn't let him do anything else? From the moment he'd held Caitlin Rose MacDonald at birth, he'd never had any choice but to love her.

Just as he'd never had any choice but to love her mother. Which was why, later this morning, he would stand at Rose's side and accept the responsibility of being Caitlin's godfather.

He turned from the window with a muttered curse, but there was nowhere he could run, nowhere he could hide from the truth. He loved her. Dear God, how had it happened? He'd been so sure he could never again feel anything but contempt for her, so sure that all he wanted from her was his ranch. He'd clung to his bitterness like it was an invincible shield, determined to guard his heart at all cost. But the woman he'd armed himself against was a money-hungry, manipulating little bitch, not a soft, vulnerable widow with wounds as deep as his. The minute he'd seen her pain, the second he'd realized that she was just as much a victim as he was, he'd lost not only the battle, but the whole stinking war. After five long years of trying to hate her, he loved her more than he'd ever thought possible.

And he didn't have a damn thing to offer her.

To some men that might not have been a problem, but the knowledge tore at him, ripping him apart. His pride was all he had left, and that was going to take a beating the moment he turned up at the church with Rose for the baby's christening. Some good-hearted soul would take one look at them together, remember their past, and wonder if he might be sniffing after her for the same reason gossips had claimed she'd married Frank so suddenly all those years ago—for the ranch.

Rose would hear the gossip, of course—she was supposed to. And there wasn't a doubt in his mind that she'd believe it. Hell, why shouldn't she? he thought bitterly. When she'd accused him of coming back for revenge, he hadn't denied it. Then it had been true. She wouldn't care that he had changed his mind, that he'd backed off after she'd had Caitlin, that it was *she* who had pursued him then, and not the other way around. She would look him straight in the eye, see that he had intended to manipulate her just as badly as Frank and her father had, and hate his guts. And he had no one to blame but himself.

So run, a voice in his head urged. Leave before you have to see the love die in her eyes. All you have to do is get in your truck and drive until you can find a place where roses don't bloom. Maybe then you'll be able to forget her and the baby.

But he couldn't. Not yet. He had promised her he'd be there for Caitlin, and come hell or high water, he would be.

Dressed in a soft lavender crepe dress with a shawl neckline, Rose hitched Caitlin higher in her arms and anxiously paced the foyer of the church. Inside the organist softly played a hymn in preparation for the service, which would start in five minutes. Her heart starting to thud with panic, Rose pivoted toward the glass doors that led to the parking lot. Maryann had arrived ten minutes ago and was already seated in the first pew, but there was no sign of Sullivan. When he'd called earlier announcing that he had some errands to do before church, he'd promised he'd be there on time. So where the heck was he? Couldn't he see that time was running out?

Her stomach knotted with tension, she tried to ignore the fear that he wasn't going to show. He wouldn't do that to her or the baby, she told herself. But she couldn't quite shake the uneasy feeling that had been with her all week. He'd been like a horse trapped in a barn with the smell of fire, ready to bolt at the first opportunity. Every time he'd turned to her, every time his eyes had met hers, she'd half expected him to flatly announce that he couldn't be the baby's godfather, that he couldn't, wouldn't love her, that he had no desire to be a part of her life. The words had never come, but with each new day she'd waited for her hopes and dreams to blow up in her face.

Where was he?

"Are you ready?"

The softly spoken question came from directly behind her and nearly buckled her knees. She whirled, tears stinging the back of her eyes at the sight of him dressed in a dark blue Western-style suit, his cowboy hat in his hand. "Sullivan, thank God! The service starts in just a few minutes and I was so afraid—"

She broke off abruptly, refusing to acknowledge the fear, but it was still there in her wide blue eyes for him to see. "My errand took longer than I expected," he explained quietly. He wanted to slip his arm around her then, to apologize with a kiss, but that would really set the gossips talking. And he didn't intend to give them any more to speculate about than he had to. Drawing his gaze from Rose, he looked down at Caitlin in her pristine white christening dress, and the love he wouldn't risk showing Rose in public was there for the baby. "Hi, angel," he growled softly. "Ready for your big day?"

The baby's face lit up with an adoring grin. "We'll know soon enough," Rose chuckled. "This is her first church service. If we're lucky, she'll sleep through the whole thing. Let's find a seat."

His hand at the back of her waist, Sullivan guided her down the aisle to the front row, where Maryann anxiously waited for them. Quickly taking seats next to her, they had hardly sat down when the minister made his way to the podium and the service began.

The organ music swelled to the rafters and the first hymn was sung, but Sullivan could still feel the surprise that had rippled through the congregation as people caught sight of him with Rose and her baby. He could still hear the hushed murmurings that had marked their progress toward the front of the church. So it had begun, he thought in disgust. The speculations, the whisperings, the gossip that was taken more seriously than the evening news. He could hear it now. Five minutes after the christening, it would be all over town that Sullivan Jones and Rose MacDonald had unabashedly walked into church together to make him her baby's godfather, and poor Frank was probably turning over in his grave. Everyone knew how he'd always hated the Joneses.

No! Sullivan swore under his breath. Damn the old biddies who had nothing better to do with their lives than pass judgment on everyone else! He could only imagine the hell they'd put Rose through five years ago, when everything she had done had been grist for the gossip mill. Without even knowing her, they'd condemned her for being young and afraid and turning to the richest man in the county because she'd thought he was her only friend. How she must have hated being the subject of every wagging tongue, her most private decisions discussed over back fences by complete strangers who neither knew nor cared about the pain she was going through. And now she was right back in the same position she'd been before. Because of him.

This was a mistake, he realized too late. Why had it taken him so long to see that? She didn't need him at her side, stirring up the past. She'd had to defend her decision to marry Frank, and now she would be forced to defend her involvement with him. And she would hate him for that. He had to leave.

Her thigh and hip pressed to his, Rose felt his turmoil, the tension that had him strung as tight as a rubber band stretched to the limit. Cradling the baby close, she shot him a worried look, but his eyes were on the minister, the rough, angled lines of his face carved in granite. She moved closer, intending to ask in a low whisper what was wrong, but she never got the chance. The minister smilingly announced the birth of Caitlin to the congregation, then motioned for Rose, Sullivan and Maryann to rise and approach the altar for the baptism.

Moments later, it was over. Caitlin never even whimpered as water was sprinkled over her head, but smiled instead, drawing a wide grin from the minister. His blessing warmly falling over her, he kissed her, congratulated Rose on having a beautiful daughter, then turned to the congregation at Rose's request and invited everyone back to the ranch for a small celebration. A murmur of approval spread through the crowd as everyone spilled from the pews into the aisles. Ranchers that had done business with her father came swarming up to see both her and Caitlin, and before she knew it, Sullivan was pulled away by an old friend of his grandfather's.

She was losing him. It was a ridiculous thought to have when she was surrounded by well-wishers and separated from him by only ten feet, but instinct warned her something was terribly wrong. Plastering a smile on her face, she thanked one of the town's nosiest gossips who was gushing over Caitlin, but her gaze immediately strayed back to Sullivan the minute the woman moved on. Somehow he was farther away than ever, though she would have sworn he hadn't moved an inch.

He pointed to the parking lot. "I'll meet you back at the ranch," he mouthed, his words drowned out by the conversation swirling around them.

Rose wanted to protest that she'd rather ride back with him so she would have a chance to ask him what was wrong, but that meant someone would have to drive her back to town later to retrieve her truck. Reluctantly she nodded and began working her way through the crowd.

* * *

Rose never knew if the huge crowd that showed up for the small party she'd planned came out of a feeling of celebration or curiosity, but within moments of her arrival back at the ranch, a string of pickups and cars pulled in behind her. Stunned, she watched guests start toward the house and knew she didn't have nearly enough food prepared to feed them. Quickly unbuckling the baby from her infant car seat, she hurried inside, desperately trying to remember what she could pull out of the freezer and heat in the microwave.

But Pop was way ahead of her. The minute she stepped through the back door, he grinned at her harried look and said, "Calm down. I've got it all under control. While you were in church, I ran into town and got a ham, some of that deli potato salad that always needs half a bottle of mustard to give it some taste, and a couple of store-bought cakes. It ain't as good as what you'd make yourself, but nobody'll go away hungry."

"What about plates? Tea? Dear God, do we have enough ice?"

She started to turn toward the freezer, but he stopped her by simply stepping in her path. "We've got plenty of ice and everything else," he assured her. "You just leave it all to me and the boys and go greet your guests. Oh, and Sullivan got home a few minutes before you did. He's waiting for you in the nursery. Said to tell you he had something for you."

Surprised, the thought of food flew right out of her head. "Something for me? What?"

He chuckled and plucked Caitlin from her arms. "Go find out. I'll take care of the little one and introduce her around. You take your time."

Rose knew she shouldn't. She needed to see if someone had found the lawn chairs and make sure Pop had remembered to put on a pot of coffee. But all she could think of was Sullivan . . . waiting for her. Unable to resist the lure, she kissed Pop's grizzly cheek and Caitlin's silky soft one and murmured, "Thanks, Pop," before flying down the hall.

The nursery door was closed, shutting out the visitors milling about the house. Soundlessly opening it, Rose slipped inside only to gasp in delight. There, by the window, sat a beautiful white Victorian wicker rocking chair that was exactly like the one she'd dreamed about, exactly like the one she'd spent months searching the Hill Country for without success. Tears filled her eyes. He'd remembered just what she wanted.

Stepping from behind the door, Sullivan saw her tremulous smile, her suspiciously bright eyes, and just barely resisted the urge to reach for her. If he held her now, he'd never be able to let her go. And that was what he was doing—letting her go before she had the chance to despise him. Forcing a rueful smile that never reached his eyes, he said, "Does that mean you love it or hate it?"

Her chuckle was watery, her eyes brilliant with love as she whirled and flew into his arms. "I love it, of course! Where did you find it? How did you know—"

Fairly dancing with happiness, she never noticed how quickly he put her away from him or how rigid his jaw was as he urged her toward the chair. "I saw it yesterday sitting on the front porch of Carla's Antique Shop down on Main Street—she'd just gotten it in. The minute I saw it, it reminded me of you. Try it out."

Sinking down to the cushioned seat, she leaned back and set the chair in motion, the fingers of her right hand lacing with his. "It's perfect," she said softly. "Just perfect. I'll keep it always."

Keepsakes. That was all she would have of him; memories were all he had to give her. Cursing his stubborn pride, he said stiffly, "You'd better get back to your guests. They're probably wondering where you are."

She didn't want to go. Just a few more minutes, she promised herself. She still needed to talk to him, to find out what was bothering him, but that was something she knew would have to wait. She could hardly hole up in the nursery with him for a serious conversation when the house was full of people. Sighing in defeat, she pushed to her feet and turned toward the door.

But in the end he couldn't let her leave, not yet. Before she could take a step away from him, he grabbed her wrist and pulled her back into his arms, his mouth immediately lowering to hers in a hot, desperate kiss of longing and regret. He felt her surprise, her shudder of need, the instant heat that had her melting against him with a moan of surrender. He could have lost it then, just that quickly lost what little control he had left where she was concerned. Her tongue dueled with his in a frantic, hungry dance, and all he could think of was pulling her to the floor and losing himself in her. Now, before she had reason to suspect every kiss and touch they'd shared since his return. Now, before he got out of her life once and for all.

But that would only prolong the agony.

The kiss turned gentle, sweet, unbearably tender. Tears stinging her eyes, Rose reluctantly let him end the kiss and draw back until the only contact between them was the tips of her fingers grazing his hard jaw. "I'll see you after the party," she whispered huskily and slipped from the room without ever seeing the despair that burned in his eyes.

The party only lasted two hours, but to Rose it seemed to drag on half the afternoon. Forcing a smile, she circulated among the guests, kept a watchful eye on the food, and retreated for a short while to the nursery to put Caitlin down for a nap. And during all that time she only caught a glimpse of Sullivan once. He was in the kitchen on his way out the back door.

She tried to tell herself that he'd gone out to join the men smoking on the back porch. After all, he'd grown up with most of them, and this was the first time he'd had to socialize since he'd come back. But as the guests started to leave and she walked out with them to thank them for coming, there was no sign of Sullivan anywhere.

Alarmed without knowing why, her gaze flew to the foreman's house down the hill. His truck was parked out back, just as it always was when he was home. She should have been relieved, but the apprehension she couldn't explain never lessened its assault on the lining of her stomach.

Turning abruptly, she went in search of Pop and found him on the back porch enjoying a cup of coffee as the last of the guests departed. "They're leaving just in time," he said, nodding toward the cars and trucks dragging dust behind them as they headed for town. "The last of the ham disappeared five minutes ago." Suddenly noting her agitation, he frowned. "What's wrong?"

"I need to talk to Sullivan at his place," she said without preamble. "Will you watch Caitlin for me? I should be back before she wakes up, but if I'm not, just call me."

He didn't even hesitate. "Course I will. Go on."

"Thanks, Pop." Giving him a quick hug, she hurried inside and grabbed her purse, then raced outside to fire up her pickup, too anxious to take the time to walk the eight hundred yards between her house and Sullivan's.

She found him in his bedroom. Packing. Stopping in the doorway, she deliberately blocked it. "I'm not letting you walk out on me again."

Sullivan jerked around to find her glaring at him, hurt and betrayal darkening her eyes and sheer gut determination setting her jaw. She wasn't going to let him go without a confrontation, he realized, and suddenly, as quickly as it took a match to ignite a firecracker, he was blazingly mad. Did she think he wanted to leave, to put them both through hell again? Last time he'd been young and stupid and too damn ignorant, and like a fool, he'd turned his back on the best thing that had ever happened to him. But this time, he knew what he was losing. Couldn't she see that it was tearing him apart?

Throwing the last of his clothes in his suitcase, he slammed it shut and turned to face her. "I've got nothing to offer you," he said coldly. "*Nothing!* And don't you dare tell me it doesn't matter," he growled when she opened her mouth to answer him. "The minute we stepped in church this morning, the gossips had a field day. Every wagging tongue in Kerrville thinks I'm after you to get my ranch back."

"Then every wagging tongue is wrong," she snapped, her blue eyes blazing. "I won't let you destroy us because of a pack of lies started by a bunch of old women who don't know what they're talking about."

"How do you know they're lies?" he taunted softly, bitterly. "Think about it, honey. I was desperate, homeless, and you had what was once mine. Can you think of an easier way for me to solve my problems than to make you fall in love with me again, then convince you to marry me?"

If he expected her to be devastated, he was in for a rude awakening. "I knew what you were planning weeks ago," she confessed. "You were hurt and angry and bitter, and I might have considered the same thing if I'd been in your shoes. But you couldn't go through with it, could you?"

She stepped toward him, unable to bear the distance between them. "That's why you stayed gone six weeks after Caitlin was born. That's why *I* was the one who had to do the seducing. If you hadn't had a change of heart, you wouldn't be packing now—you'd be begging me to marry you.''

"Considering that my only asset is a beat-up old pickup truck, what other way could I convince a woman to marry me than by begging?"

Rose winced at the bitterness of his tone, wishing with all her heart she could have spared him the humiliation of losing his ranch. Fumbling with the clasp of her purse, she drew out the papers she had been carrying around for weeks and held them out to him. "I believe this belongs to you."

He looked down blankly at the folded paper, then back up at her. Watching the emotions flickering across his face, Rose held her breath as he gingerly took the legal document and opened it. An instant later his narrowed gaze snapped up to hers. "This is the deed to the Lazy J."

"Yes. I had it put in your name while you were on the cattle-buying trip after the baby was born. I was waiting for a chance to give it to you when you wouldn't throw it back in my face."

His mind reeling, Sullivan could only stare at her. "Why?"

"Because it's yours," she said simply. "The Lazy J has always belonged to the Joneses. Frank was wrong to take it, to set your father up the way he did. When I found out about it, I tried to stop him, but he was determined to have it. If your father had let you come home when you wanted to, none of this would have ever happened."

His fingers curled around the paper, gripping it as if he were afraid it would disappear. "Why now?" he asked hoarsely. "Why are you giving this to me now?"

It was a question he had every right to ask. She could see by the look in his eye, that he, too, realized what a risk she was taking. He had what he'd come for, what he'd practically sold his soul for to get back. He could leave without a backward glance and there wouldn't be a thing she could do to stop him.

But the future she knew they could have together was worth any gamble. "Because I love you," she said quietly. "Once before I lost you because of misunderstandings and other people's interference. This time there can be no doubts. No misunderstandings. If you walk away from me, it can be for no other reason than you don't love me. That's the only excuse you have left, the only excuse I'll accept."

"And if I stay?" he growled softly.

"It can be for no other reason than you love me," she replied, repeating herself but for one crucial word. "That's the only excuse you have left, the only excuse I'll accept."

So this was it, do or die, the choice totally and completely his. But it was a choice he had made years ago, a choice that he had, during endless winter nights, often bitterly regretted and tried his damnedest to deny, a choice he was finally forced to admit he couldn't run away from. From the moment he'd first laid eyes on her when she was seventeen, he'd loved her.

His eyes locked with hers, he took a step *toward*, not away from, her. "Do you really think I could walk away from you a second time?"

Her knees would have totally given way in relief then if he hadn't reached for her and hauled her into his arms. "Say it," she whispered, aching. "I need to hear you say it."

He groaned, pulling her closer. "Oh, sweetheart, don't you know that I say it every time I kiss you? Every time I touch you?" Tenderly capturing her face in his hands, he tilted her chin up until he could gaze down into the deep sapphire pools of her eyes. "Let me translate," he mumbled. "This—" he pressed a feather-soft kiss to each eye "—means I love you. This—" his voice deepened to a low sexy growl as his lips covered hers for a long, precious, heart-stealing moment filled with promises "—means I adore you. Always. And this—" he reached for her left hand and gently ran his thumb over her bare ring finger "—means I don't ever want to face another day without you or Caitlin at my side. Marry me," he urged thickly. "Take my name and my heart and promise me nothing will ever come between us again."

She crowded closer. "Oh, yes."

Just that simply, she gave herself into his keeping. Sullivan felt his throat fill with emotion, choking him. Wrapping his arms around her, binding her to him as if he would never let her go, he said huskily, "I want to adopt Caitlin."

Her eyes blurred, a brilliant smile lighting her face. She would have never asked that of him—to claim as his own the child of a man who tried to destroy his family—but it was the one thing she hadn't dared to let herself hope for that would make everything perfect. Rising on tiptoe, she kissed him with a tenderness that sent the tears welling in her eyes spilling over, telling him without a single word of the happiness she couldn't express. "That will make it perfect," she said softly. "In every way that counts, she's been yours from the moment she was born. You're going to be a wonderful father."

He wanted to believe it, but every time he thought of being a father, he thought of his own. "My own wasn't exactly a prime candidate for father of the year," he reminded her quietly.

She drew back to look at him in surprise. "No, but your grandfather was. I remember you telling me stories of how he taught you to ride and hunt, and how you'd spend hours together down at that old cypress tree at the bend of the river trying to catch the granddaddy of all catfish. You were crazy about that old man. Just like Caitlin and our other kids are going to be crazy about you."

She sounded so sure, so indignant that he could possibly think otherwise, he couldn't help but grin. "You think so, huh?"

She nodded, her blue eyes dancing. "Of course, I'm a pretty terrific mother, too. Between the two of us, our kids can't lose."

"No, sweetheart," he murmured, lowering his mouth to claim hers. "Between the two of us, *we* can't lose!"

* * * * *

MILLION DOLLAR JACKPOT
SWEEPSTAKES RULES & REGULATIONS
NO PURCHASE NECESSARY TO ENTER OR RECEIVE A PRIZE

1. Alternate means of entry: Print your name and address on a 3" ×5" piece of plain paper and send to the appropriate address below.

In the U.S.	**In Canada**
MILLION DOLLAR JACKPOT	MILLION DOLLAR JACKPOT
P.O. Box 1867	P.O. Box 609
3010 Walden Avenue	Fort Erie, Ontario
Buffalo, NY 14269-1867	L2A 5X3

2. To enter the Sweepstakes and join the Reader Service, affix the Four Free Books and Free Gifts sticker along with both of your other Sweepstakes stickers to the Sweepstakes Entry Form. If you do not wish to take advantage of our Reader Service, but wish to enter the Sweepstakes only, do not affix the Four Free Books and Free Gifts sticker; affix only the Sweepstakes stickers to the Sweepstakes Entry Form. Incomplete and/or inaccurate entries are ineligible for that section or sections of prizes. Torstar Corp. and its affiliates are not responsible for mutilated or unreadable entries or inadvertent printing errors. Mechanically reproduced entries are null and void.

3. Whether you take advantage of this offer or not, on or about April 30, 1992, at the offices of D.L. Blair, Inc., Blair, NE, your sweepstakes numbers will be compared against the list of winning numbers generated at random by the computer. However, prizes will only be awarded to individuals who have entered the Sweepstakes. In the event that all prizes are not claimed, a random drawing will be held from all qualified entries received from March 30, 1990 to March 31, 1992, to award all unclaimed prizes. All cash prizes (Grand to Sixth) will be mailed to winners and are payable by check in U.S. funds. Seventh prize will be shipped to winners via third-class mail. These prizes are in addition to any free, surprise or mystery gifts that might be offered. Versions of this Sweepstakes with different prizes of approximate equal value may appear at retail outlets or in other mailings by Torstar Corp. and its affiliates.

4. PRIZES: (1) *Grand Prize $1,000,000.00 Annuity; (1) First Prize $25,000.00; (1) Second Prize $10,000.00; (5) Third Prize $5,000.00; (10) Fourth Prize $1,000.00; (100) Fifth Prize $250.00; (2,500) Sixth Prize $10.90; (6,000) **Seventh Prize $12.95 ARV.

   *This presentation offers a Grand Prize of a $1,000,000.00 annuity. Winner will receive $33,333.33 a year for 30 years without interest totalling $1,000,000.00.

   **Seventh Prize: A fully illustrated hardcover book, published by Torstar Corp. Approximate Retail Value of the book is $12.95. Entrants may cancel the Reader Service at any time without cost or obligation (see details in Center Insert Card).

5. Extra Bonus! This presentation offers an Extra Bonus Prize valued at $33,000.00 to be awarded in a random drawing from all qualified entries received by March 31, 1992. No purchase necessary to enter or receive a prize. To qualify, see instructions in Center Insert Card. Winner will have the choice of any of the merchandise offered or a $33,000.00 check payable in U.S. funds. All other published rules and regulations apply.

6. This Sweepstakes is being conducted under the supervision of D.L. Blair, Inc. By entering the Sweepstakes, each entrant accepts and agrees to be bound by these rules and the decisions of the judges, which shall be final and binding. Odds of winning the random drawing are dependent upon the number of entries received. Taxes, if any, are the sole responsibility of the winners. Prizes are nontransferable. All entries must be received at the address on the detachable Business Reply Card and must be postmarked no later than 12:00 MIDNIGHT on March 31, 1992. The drawing for all unclaimed Sweepstakes prizes and for the Extra Bonus Prize will take place on May 30, 1992, at 12:00 NOON at the offices of D.L. Blair, Inc., Blair, NE.

7. This offer is open to residents of the U.S., United Kingdom, France and Canada, 18 years or older, except employees and immediate family members of Torstar Corp., its affiliates, subsidiaries and all other agencies, entities and persons connected with the use, marketing or conduct of this Sweepstakes. All Federal, State, Provincial, Municipal and local laws apply. Void wherever prohibited or restricted by law. Any litigation within the Province of Quebec respecting the conduct and awarding of a prize in this publicity contest must be submitted to the Régie des Loteries et Courses du Québec.

8. Winners will be notified by mail and may be required to execute an affidavit of eligibility and release, which must be returned within 14 days after notification or an alternate winner may be selected. Canadian winners will be required to correctly answer an arithmetical, skill-testing question administered by mail, which must be returned within a limited time. Winners consent to the use of their name, photograph and/or likeness for advertising and publicity in conjunction with this and similar promotions without additional compensation.

9. For a list of our major prize winners, send a stamped, self-addressed envelope to: MILLION DOLLAR WINNERS LIST, P.O. Box 4510, Blair, NE 68009. Winners Lists will be supplied after the May 30, 1992 drawing date.

Offer limited to one per household.

LTY-S791

SILHOUETTE·INTIMATE·MOMENTS®

IT'S TIME TO MEET
THE MARSHALLS!

In 1986, bestselling author Kristin James wrote A VERY SPECIAL FAVOR for the Silhouette Intimate Moments line. Hero Adam Marshall quickly became a reader favorite, and ever since then, readers have been asking for the stories of his two brothers, Tag and James. At last your prayers have been answered!

In August, look for THE LETTER OF THE LAW (IM #393), James Marshall's story. If you missed youngest brother Tag's story, SALT OF THE EARTH (IM #385), you can order it by following the directions below. And, as our very special favor to you, we'll be reprinting A VERY SPECIAL FAVOR this September. Look for it in special displays wherever you buy books.

Silhouette Books®